Fire's

Revenge

Jeni Burns

Media Jam, LLC
15105-D John J. Delaney Drive; #317
Charlotte, NC 28277
www.jeniburns.com
Publisher's Note: This is a work of fiction. Names, characters, places, and incidents are a product of the author's imagination. Locales and public names are sometimes used for atmospheric purposes. Any resemblance to actual people, living or dead, or to businesses, companies, events, institutions, or locales is completely coincidental.

Cover Design: Michelle Fairbanks. Fresh Design

Fire's Revenge/ Jeni Burns. – 2nd ed.

ISBN: 1942964056
ISBN-13: 978-1-942964-05-6

To the original Elma,

I always thought your name was perfect.

All my love.

I. OVERWORLD - CIRCA 1725

Playing Fate is like playing the house. The house always wins; that is, until someone comes in and burns the house to the ground.
- Random Thought #7,950

Fate knew her job as pseudo-deity was important and she performed it dutifully. That was until one half-devil, half-witch waltzed into the Overworld uninvited and stole a precious artifact.

With a charming smile and some smooth talking, the young devil-witch dazzled Fate. It had been so long since the last time she had actually conversed with another. The idea of a visit from a being that could cross between the Overworld and Underworld plucked on her heartstrings, playing them like a master composer.

Their time together was brief. In his first visit she only learned his name: Drammelech; Elech as his family called him. She offered Elech her title in lieu of her name: Fate. He flashed her a wide smile with the hint of a dimple at its corner and said she must have known he'd come for her. Fate laughed off his flirty nature and relished the time they spoke.

He brought her a single fluffy pink flower on his next visit.

"What is this?"

"Rue."

"Rue? Why would you bring me something with such a sad connotation?" Fate studied the young man before her.

"Because I rue that I cannot have you in my everyday life. Your beauty speaks to me in a way that nothing in my realm ever has." His bashful eyes lowered, punctuating his proclamation with the light stain of red that colored his cheeks.

It was in that simple confession that her heart filled as it never had before. She took great pains to make sure every moment of their time together was well spent, full of laughter, conversation, and genuine happiness. On one particular visit, Elech asked to see more than the main chamber of her Overworld post. She didn't hesitate to take him into her most favorite room—

the records room.

Fate led him into the vault where all living beings' scrolls were kept under lock and key. It reminded her of the warehouses that her charges used to store useless baubles and tokens. The difference was that the vault was unending.

The day she had taken over for the previous soul, Fate was shown into this very chamber of vastness that seemed larger than anything she could comprehend. She recalled asking in a hushed tone how big the chamber was. The look on her predecessor's face was answer enough and no more words were needed.

In all her years in the Overworld, Fate had yet to figure out the magical system to the order of the scrolls. The easiest to find belonged to the mystical beings who lived among the humans. Those scrolls always appeared near the front of the shelves and often had brightly colored symbols on the exterior of the rolled parchment.

With every falling grain of sand in the constantly flowing hourglass that mimicked the time of her charges, new scrolls would appear while others would disappear. However, each new scroll looked like it had always been there. Fate oftentimes wondered if the disappearing scrolls reappeared elsewhere in the cavernous chamber. But she never ventured forth in search of them because it would take longer than she could spare. If her back was turned for a moment, turmoil could erupt amongst her charges since time in the Overworld didn't work the same as it did on Earth.

Even with that sense of urgency always on her mind, her forays into this chamber were typically the highlight of her time spent in the Overworld.

Fate stepped aside and allowed Elech entrance into this sacred space. It gave her a sense of joy to share this place with someone. The majestic nature of it never failed to take her breath away. Fate wanted so much to share her joy with Elech. She watched, rapt, as a wash of emotions rolled over his handsome face and settled in his piercing eyes.

"What is this place?" Awe laced every word.

"I call it the chamber of records." She fingered the delicate shell of the hourglass. "This is where the universe is balanced. The scrolls strike a tenuous balance between light and dark, old and new, beginnings and endings."

Elech walked farther into the room and ran a hand along a shelf housing mounds of scrolls. His fingers settled on one and slipped it from the shelf. With a gentle hand, he unrolled the parchment and scanned it.

"What if this scroll was misplaced?" He rerolled it and held the rolled parchment between his thumb and forefinger like it might burn him.

"It mustn't." Fate moved toward him and snatched the scroll from his grasp. "This single scroll represents the life of one of my charges and if something were to happen, another scroll would surely appear to maintain the balance." She gently slid the scroll back into its place on the shelf.

Elech nodded and walked back to the main

opening in the chamber. Beside the hourglass was a podium that held the largest tome the world never knew existed. Its leather wrapped spine was the glue that held all of Earth's existence together. Tucked into the pages of the book laid a blade: Fate's dagger, the most powerful item in the chamber. Her predecessor had gone to great lengths to reiterate the importance of keeping it hidden away, and Fate was mindful of that as Elech drew closer and closer to its resting place. An item of such power in the wrong hands could cause so much damage in the world, but in Fate's hands it was the instrument to correct things gone awry. As Elech inspected the hourglass, a sigh left her lips.

Fate watched the steady trickle of sand and moved to her left. She fingered the thick leather-bound tome that was home to a long list of names and slid the jeweled silver hilt from between the book's pages. It felt heavy in her hand as she tucked it into the garter beneath her long flowing skirt. Knowing the blade was safe gave Fate a sense of peace.

Elech's next visit was years later though the time passed seemingly in the blink of an eye. This time he appeared a full grown man even though she knew his age to be young by her charges' standards. Instead of another pink fluffy rue, he held in his hand a long stemmed white rose.

"I thought you might've forgotten me," she remarked as she accepted his offering.

"Never."

His voice was deep, full-bodied, and sent a

chill racing down her spine. When his hands slid down her arms, an actual shiver sliced through her body. How long had it been since she had felt the touch of another? Long before being assigned to her current post, that's for sure. She arched into him, pleased to find him hard and angular beneath her wanton fingers. In the space of a breath he had her in his arms, hands scorching over her exposed skin until fabric balled into his eager hands. His mouth, warm on her chaste lips, tasted like sunshine and a warm summer's breeze.

Fate threw caution and dignity into the wind and succumbed to Elech. With each tantalizing touch of his fingers against her flesh, she basked in the sensations of seduction. The fluttering in her chest, an anomaly that could almost be mistaken for a heartbeat, kicked up as his tentative touches became more determined on their trail up her thighs and beneath her skirt. She closed her eyes and cherished the intimacy of her predicament until a tug sent her eyes wide. The cool blade of the dagger she wore in the garter against her thigh sliced though her delicate flesh in a rush of warm, sticky liquid. Before she could defend herself, the press of the blade against her throat halted any further movement.

"I hate to do this," Elech whispered in her ear. "But you are the only thing standing between me and greatness." He pressed his lips to hers in a final kiss as the blade dug into her skin once more, this time slicing across her throat until it became hard to breathe. The fluttering in her chest that made her more human than ethereal catapulted, racing toward a finish line she could no longer sense. Elech stood, wiped the broad side of the blade against his trousers and blinked out of the realm.

Without Fate to dictate the course of human existence, chaos was sure to ensue. Protecting her charges from whatever evil Elech planned was more important. With her last breaths, Fate dragged herself into the chamber of records and sealed the doors behind her with all of her remaining magic. Now Elech would need more than just his smooth words to get into the chamber. Satisfied with her fortitude and forethought, Fate crumpled into a heap on the floor, knocking scrolls about on her way down. As much as she wanted to retrieve them and put them right again, she no longer had the strength. Fate stared at the scattered rolls of parchment decorated with symbols she knew instinctively. The mess on the floor would surely change the course of life for her beloved charges, but how, she could only guess.

A last thought flashed through her brain as the fading embers of light in her soul flickered out. "What have I done?"

2. EARTH – PRESENT DAY

Star light, star bright, first star I see tonight… No wait. That's a…*Ka-Boom*
- Random Thought # 3,928

∿

Yawning only begot more yawning and Elms McMillan was already seven yawns deep into the paper she'd neglected to start writing until the very last minute. If she didn't get this in on time, the risk of failing out of her nursing program would quickly become a reality that she didn't want to face. The ornate grandfather clock in the corner of the dining room chimed the desolate hour of half past two in the morning, each note mocking her procrastinating heart. The cursor blinked, adding its own rhythmic taunts. Ugh.

A flash of light, too bright to be natural through the curtains drawn across the dining room window, caught her eye. Winter in New Jersey wasn't the typical season for rogue thunderstorms, so when the clash of thunder followed with not a cloud nor a hint of rain in the night sky, Elms knew this wasn't a natural atmospheric disturbance. Add to it the fact that her eye could only track one bright streak of embers, and it solidified in her mind that this wasn't some kids playing with off-season fireworks. And it sure as heck wasn't another excuse to postpone her assignment. No. Intuition spelled out that something was wrong with her newest patient, and it was her responsibility to fix it.

It was only natural that her first-ever patient would be explosive, because that was how Fate played with Elms. Convinced that she was the butt of some cosmic joke that Fate told on repeat, Elms slammed closed her laptop and made her way toward the front of the house.

"Craptastic," she muttered. Her heartbeat marched a double-time staccato as she snatched an afghan from the back of the couch, careful not to disturb her aunt who was watching late-night reruns through her eyelids.

"Elms? Are you heading up to bed?" Aunt Sue's voice was thick with sleep.

"I didn't mean to wake you." Elms leaned over the back of the couch and planted a gentle kiss on her aunt's cheek. "Looks like a storm is coming in. And I'm pretty sure the storm's name is Tiffy."

Another flash lit the sky. Elms wrapped the afghan over her nightie and headed for the door in her favorite fluffy unicorn slippers.

"Good luck, dear. I have faith that you'll be able to help her this time," Sue called out as the door clicked closed.

"I hope so, cause last time didn't work out so well," she said, grumbling to the night sky.

With the memory of her aunt's favorite rosebush going up in flames, thanks to Tiffy's combustive nature, Elms concentrated on shifting the molecules of her human form into that of her Elemental nature. Within seconds her body ceased to exist, her cells separating, twisting, mutating into the opal-hued cloud that was her element: Wind.

The air around her vibrated with the tension of her change—tugging, toying, tormenting—as she flew toward The Outpost. Her flight was turbulent at best, and the flashes in the sky were getting more frequent with every passing minute. Elms fought against the tumbling wind around her, determined that this time she would be able to successfully help her first patient.

She glided over the wooded, mountainous terrain that made up the small farm town of Harmony. Far from the exits of the notorious turnpike, Harmony was a safe haven for the members of the Elemental community. Land acted as a natural barrier between neighbors, yet still allowed a sense of community between the humans and Elementals that inhabited the town. Living in the sticks had its advantages. Neighbors weren't close enough to be nosey and farmers were oblivious to the supernatural goings ons. The camouflage of living in small town America allowed for the secretive Elementals to hide in plain sight.

Elms' conscience was all too aware that if her patient continued these explosive outbursts, the humans in Harmony might start asking questions. And the first rule of being an Elemental was to keep the Elementals a secret from the humans. That rule was the only thing keeping the supernatural race from being hunted, persecuted, and wiped off the face of the Earth.

She neared the only bar in town and headed for the parking lot which happened epicenter of the heated flashes of light shooting into the sky. The Outpost's neon lights glowed in the barred windows and cast funky colors on the crocus planted in old water troughs lining the front of the red brick building.

Elms merged her consciousness with her pulsing molecules and took her human form. The only fabrics that her wind nature had held was the worn afghan and the slippers, which was better than nothing as that was often what her essence held. She wrapped the afghan around her shoulders, blocking out the cold and hiding her nakedness from any wandering eyes that might still be awake.

Elms cringed when another trumpet of thunder crashed overhead. A flash of lightning punctuated the pristine serenity of the night. Nerves frayed to the very edge, Elms took a deep

11

breath to gather her calm then yelled Tiffy's name to the heavens. When she was met with more exploding embers of heat in the sky, her patience waned.

"Come on, Tiffy. I know you can hear me. I'm here to help you." She stomped her foot in a show of frustration and hugged the afghan tighter to her small frame, but gooseflesh pebbled her chilled skin. Snow warmed under her feet, but the longer she stayed put, the colder her feet became. "Look, you and I both know you'd rather have someone else treating you for this, but I'm all you've got." She waved her hand from head to waist to drive her point home. "Now, get your fanny down here so we can both get on with our night."

Elms could feel the shift in the air around her when her words connected with Tiffy's consciousness. The streak of light gathered until it coiled in on itself and became a single ball of fire. Absent of the heat required to produce the thunderous noise, the night quieted. The dimming fireball began an acrobatic descent toward the snow-covered gravel parking lot of the bar.

Elms' patient, Tiffy—a Fire Elemental and local mixer of all things alcoholic, took the shape of a human-sized ball of fire. Long legs, slender arms, and the kind of curves women had surgery to attain began to emerge. A few last flames licked the creamy surface of her moonlight-kissed skin.

"What took you so long?" the blond waitress asked, her voice raw with frustration. "I've been exploding for almost a half hour. You told me you'd come right away to break whatever cycle triggers this." The pout on Tiffy's face yanked at Elms' heart, leaving a sting of anxiety prickling down her legs.

Elms watched graceful curls of smoke waft from the melting snow beneath her patient's feet. "I got here as soon as I could. Why didn't you call me before you went off?"

"I barely had the time to salvage my clothes," Tiffy said, gesturing to a duffel bag perched on the edge of a bench by the front door of the bar. She snuffed flickers of flame that continued to spring up on her arms and legs with her hands.

"Care to tell me what set you off tonight?" Elms asked, while edging closer to Tiffy to capitalize on the warmth wafting off her.

"Well, it could've been the obnoxious, beer-filled asshole who propositioned me tonight. Can you believe he did so with my parents' blessing? No, wait, maybe it was the guy who looked like he exclusively ate jelly donuts and hit on me because his drunk idiot of a friend told him I'm on the lookout for my mate."

"So stress set you off. That I can help with."

"Stress isn't the problem." The blond smoothed her hair into a ponytail and twisted it into a knot at the back of her head. "My problem is that Sophie's out of town and I have to wait for you to 'research' what's making me explode. When will the real healer be back?"

Elms flinched at the verbal barb and its

accompanying glare. She tried to swallow and choked on the dryness in her mouth. Tiffy had every right to be annoyed. As a Wind, Elms didn't have much experience in dealing with Fires, and even though her mentor taught her the basics of all the Elemental sects, there hadn't been a lesson on exploding Fires. Of course, it was her luck that her very first solo patient as a healer, apprentice or not, would bust out in flames. Why couldn't that have waited until her mentor was back in town? Because Fate had a sick sense of humor. That's why.

"I get it. Stress seems like a stupid answer, but your aura begs to differ. And I know you don't want to believe speed dating every eligible Fire in a five-state radius is stressful, but we both know that it is."

Tiffy shook her head and set loose her blond locks. "Look, if I could get away with not meeting every Homer and Dilbert-esque character on the East coast, I would, but my parents are sick of waiting for me to find my mate. My younger sister won't find hers until I find mine. You know how it works."

Elms turned her back on Tiffy, mostly to avoid her murderous glare, but also to gain control of her insecurities. It wasn't enough that Fate had given her the gift to intuit the root cause of disease among Elementals and humans, she'd also bestowed Elms with a wicked case of the heebie-jeebies when she saw blood, vomit, or any other bodily fluids belonging on the inside of someone's body. That was beyond bad, but for Fate to send her the most difficult patient she could muster while Elms' mentor was out of town and unreachable, well, that was just plain mean.

The sound of snow sizzling pulled Elms from her reverie and brought her back to Tiffy's exploding problem. She peeked over her shoulder and watched Tiffy stumble through the snow toward the duffel bag, snow melting quickly under her superheated feet.

"I can get that for you," Elms offered. Tiffy froze while Elms moved across the snow with ease as a metallic chirping cut the silence of the night.

"Shit," Tiffy said. "That's probably my mother wondering what all the fireworks were about."

Elms grabbed the bag then hurried back to Tiffy. The licks of flame retreated from the Fire's skin until the phone started its chirping again. Smoke wafted from the depth of the duffle as Tiffy tore through it with a curse. After one last chirp, she emerged with the offending device in hand.

"Shit," she said again, her shoulders deflating. "Two missed calls. She's gonna give me hell for that." The metal casing of the cell phone glowed red in her hand.

"Ugh, Tiffy..." Elms pointed to the phone and her afghan slid from her shoulder.

"What now?" The Fire whined, exasperation leaking out with each syllable.

"Your phone..." Sparks flew from the handset in every direction as the innards of the cell phone fried in her client's hand.

"Shit!" Tiffy tossed it to the ground. "That's the second one this month." Her face crumpled. "It's not stress, Elma. It can't be. I've been stressed before and this has never happened."

"Then maybe it's your mate. I've heard that once you meet your fated mate, weird things can start happening..." Elms allowed her words trail off as she wracked her brain for another explanation. Any other explanation.

"I've met no less than one hundred men over the last month and a half—most of which were of the old, balding, and beer-belly variety. If that didn't stress me out enough to explode, then I don't know why I would now." Tiffy scooped a handful of snow from the ground and slid the melting slush over one arm then repeated the motions with the other.

"Okay, let's go over it again. What's different now? I mean, when you came to me earlier this week, you said it was the first time you'd..." The word 'exploded' died on Elms' lips, "... *had* this issue." Yeah, that sounded more professional.

"Nothing's different," she shouted, throwing her hands in the air. The movement underscored Tiffy's naked-as-a-new-babe figure. "Unless you mean, my life's going to shit. Because then, that's it. My whole effing world has gone to hell. In. One. Big. Flaming, Basket. Of. Shit. Does that help?"

Sarcasm wasn't going to help, but at least her patient remained flameless. She could cross anger off the list of possible underlying causes.

"I know you said you don't think you met your mate, but maybe it's worth considering. We could run down the list of people you've met this week just in case one of them is the trigger." Elms looked hopefully at her patient and shivered in the chill that surrounded her, now that Tiffy was no longer giving off heat.

"Well, before I came to meet you on Tuesday, I'd spoken with a woman from Long Island who wanted to arrange a meeting with her twin. After that, my mom brought home a red wedding dress." Tiffy ran her hands over her body. Seemingly satisfied with the temperature of her skin, she reached into her bag, pulled out clothes, and began dressing.

"Your mom bought a wedding dress? Already?"`

"Yup. She's determined to have me mated before the end of the month when I turn thirty." The words were muffled by the pink wool of the sweater Tiffy pulled over her head.

"Brings me back to stress, I'm afraid." Elms twirled a strand of her long red hair around her finger. It was her go-to coping mechanism when she had a difficult problem before her. "Why don't you come to the office tomorrow and I can run some tests to see if we can reproduce the problem." It wasn't an answer, but it was the best she could come up with this late at night.

Tiffy paused mid-wiggle. "So, you're planning to burn Sophie's house down to prove me wrong that stress is the cause of all this?"

Elms could see Tiffy's brow raise in the poorly lit parking lot and knew the Fire was losing patience. "No one's burning down Sophie's house. The clinic has a special fire-proof room for things like this."

"Whatever you say, doc." Tiffy wrestled her jeans over her hips with a final wiggle and fastened them. She stuffed her feet into a pair of tennis shoes then hitched the bag onto her shoulder. She plucked the charred phone from the snow and tossed it in the bag. "I'll stop by in the afternoon, because I have to meet with the woman from Long Island and her brother at eleven."

Elms rubbed at her temple where the start of a headache pulsed behind her right eye. "Can we set a time? I have class tomorrow that I can't afford to keep missing."

"Whatever." Tiffy shrugged. "Let's do ten thirty because I have to bolt before eleven so I can strike one more name off my list." Tiffy crunched across the lot to a jacked-up pickup and climbed into the cab before slamming the door.

The sound of animals scurrying in the woods reached Elms' ears as the engine roared to life. The truck peeled out of the lot, spraying a shower of gravel in its wake.

"Craptastic." She brushed bits of gravel off her body and glared at the fading taillights. It was easy to understand Tiffy's frustration, but that didn't make it an easier pill to swallow—all things considered. Elms watched the taillights fade into the darkness and weighed her options. In the morning, she'd head to class and turn in her paper. Then she'd sneak out early so she could get to Sophie's with time to look through her library for anything that might shed some light on Tiffy's situation. No pun intended.

Before Elms could shift, a deep voice drifted from the shadows, chilling her to the bone.

"That was one helluva show."

3.

If a wolf in sheep's clothing is still a wolf, then the same must be true for a sheep in wolf's clothing. Right? - Random Thought # 17

∿

"Who's there?" Elms called, trying to pinpoint the direction of the mysterious voice. The silence of the night was her only answer. "Show yourself this minute!" She puffed out her chest and hoped her small frame would appear bigger and more intimidating.

"Or what? Would you dare come into the deep, dark woods to find me?"

His haunting voice rolled over her skin leaving gooseflesh in its wake. The laughter surrounded her as it echoed off the, building into an entity of its own. Her heart kicked into high gear as the instinct to flee took over. But it was unbridled fear that kept her feet rooted to the semi-frozen ground and called to her Wind nature. Fear always trumped other emotions in the hierarchy of her survival skills—limited though they were.

The night wind, at her command, shifted and rustled the bare trees like fingers sifting through sand in search of a shell. It combed through the darkness inch-by-inch at her command until the man laughed again. The wind stilled and silence descended heavy and sure.

"I give up." Laughter emerged from the woods once more. "How is it that a red-head with your temper is a Wind? Seems more fitting for a Fire."

His amused tone didn't escape her notice.

On the far side of the lot, a dark figure emerged from the tree line and stopped. Transfixed, she waited and watched, but he didn't move any closer.

"Show yourself." Her words, a prayer-like whisper, slipped from her lips as she squinted at the space where the dim bulbs of the parking lot lighting couldn't reach. Even squinting, she could only make out the basic shape of a man.

He stood maybe six feet, maybe slightly smaller. His build wasn't lean, but it wasn't bulky either. Elm's vague impression of him from this far away was that he was average. And even though he taunted her with his words, she couldn't divine an ounce of malice behind them. On second inspection, she found the opposite.

If he moved closer, Elms was sure she could get a better read on his intentions. That was one of the perks of her particular gift. The gooseflesh resurfaced when a cold gust of air rushed past her. A shiver stole her concentration.

"Are you sure you want me to show myself? Isn't the mystery more fun?"

His teasing tone wrapped around her like a velvet cloak, warmed her, and stroked every nerve ending to full alert. Her awareness of the stranger toyed around in her mind. Her heart. Her traitorous body. Something about him pulled her in, despite the adrenaline spike from baring all to a complete stranger in the middle of the night.

Her teeth chattered while she considered her answer. "I'm not a fan of mysteries. I prefer knowing what I'm up against from the start, when given the chance."

"Are you scared or just cold?"

"Cold." It was none of his darn business that she was a little scared. He had already pegged her for a Wind, which meant he at least knew about the community. But that didn't calm her nerves. Instead, it set them further on edge when the stranger chuckled.

"I'll pretend to believe you, but only if you promise to do the same when I tell you why I'm here. I'm not in the mood to be tossed out on one of your gusts."

She considered his words. "I'd agree to

those terms, but I'm not sure I can. I find it hard to trust someone afraid to show me his face." She held her breath and waited. The seconds ticked by and another shiver shook her.

"You drive a hard bargain."

The shadow man took slow steps out of the woods and into the lot. As he passed under one of the light posts, Elm's breath caught in her throat. He was perfection: dark hair, broad shoulders, and facial scruff that looked intentionally unkempt on his strong jaw. She ached to see more, especially his eyes. Those would tell her everything she needed to know.

"I think you misunderstood the terms of our agreement," she called, "I still can't see your face."

He moved even closer to where Elms was rooted to the ground. He lifted his hand and a flame rose straight from his palm, sending the shadows running.

"Better now? Or should I light the other one too?"

A small diamond stud sparkled in his ear closest to the flame. Blue eyes twinkled at her in the firelight, and a smile pulled at full lips cushioned between what she could now see was a trimmed mustache and goatee combo. Short brown hair the color of melted milk chocolate mingled with his overall features to create a picture of gentle confidence. He wore black jeans with a long trench coat and boots.

The closer he walked, the taller he appeared. With his height and wide shoulders, she was certain he could overpower her with little effort if he so chose. Another shiver scrambled up her spine, this one at the thought of being overpowered by the stranger drawing closer still.

"Still cold? Or are you ready to admit you're scared?"

The smoothness of his voice matched the visage before her. *Goddess.* He stole the breath from her very lungs.

"So, scared it is. What if I told you I was here to do recon on a woman my family is trying to set me up with? Would that make me less scary?"

Elms considered his words, weighing them against her better judgment.

"Considering it's got to be almost three a.m. and you're hiding in the dark, I'd say it makes you creepy," she finally admitted. She forced herself to look away from his knowing eyes.

He chuckled. "I can see how that might seem creepy. What if I plead insanity? Would that make it any better?"

"No." She laughed in spite of it all. "I'm pretty sure when the creepy guy pleads insanity it makes things worse..."

"Okay, okay. I get it. I'm the creepy guy who spied on the girl he's supposed to meet while she combusted out in the open where anyone could see her. And maybe I'm the guy who got a pretty good look at her when she touched back down." His wolfish smile negated the sheepish tone in his voice. "So what's a Wind doing here?"

"Well, it's... it's..." She paused. Was there

really an explanation owed here? He was a perfect stranger, after all. Sure, he admitted to being a peeping Tom, but he hadn't offered up his name or anything of a personal nature. Besides, what man in his right mind waited until the middle of the night to check out the woman he was supposed to meet? Even in the somewhat offbeat culture full of bizarre rituals and rules that the Elementals lived by, this was out of the ordinary. "It's none of your business. I'm a friend of a friend and that's all you need to know." She jutted out her chin and hoped it sold the stubborn look she was aiming for. Of course, anyone who knew her could bust that facade wide open in an instant, but he didn't know that. As long as she could sell Fire Guy on the idea that she was tough as nails—maybe not nails, bones was a better comparison—she could shift and breeze away without further incident.

"No harm meant. Just curious why a Fire and Wind were together. From what I've been told, the two don't usually mix. Unless... Were you adding a little fuel to her fire? A little gusto to her flame? A little pick-me-up to her flicker?"

The flame in his hand intensified, amplifying his chiseled features and the return of his smile—one that made her wonder if he would burn her alive given the chance.

"I... I..." she stuttered. His eyes danced with licks of flame. When their eyes met, heat rushed throughout her and every word flew right out of her mind.

"Was that it? Were you here to help her

blow off a little steam? Isn't that dangerous, Little Wind? Or do you like playing with fire?" He raised an eyebrow and moved closer. "Is that it? You like to play with fire?"

The heat radiating off him reached out and sizzled over her bit by bit until it reached her cheeks. She couldn't decide if the resulting flush was from his heat or his words. Something about his words plucked a chord deep inside. She tried to find a retort that would quiet him, but not a single word entered her brain.

Swell. Figures her brain would leave her high and dry when all she needed was something to put out a Fire.

"Sign me up, Little Wind. I'd give my right fireball to have you stoke my flame."

Now he was so close that Elms was afraid to move out of fear she'd be burned by his flame. Her knees turned to rubber as another shiver ran through her. The flame in his palm was extinguished as he closed his hand.

"Don't be afraid, Little Wind. I won't hurt you."

With an unexpected gentleness, he brushed a loose strand of hair away from her face. She held her breath and watched his hand the hand that had so easily conjured fire trail a whisper-soft descent down her bare arm. His touch was feather light on her skin, but an inferno blazed along her nerve endings chasing each point of contact. Nothing so brand new had ever felt so familiar in all her twenty-one years. Like a lost piece of her had returned after a long voyage.

She sucked in a breath, stepped back, and tripped. Grace wasn't her middle name, so when she flailed her arms to catch herself, her afghan fluttered from her shoulders and bared all.

"Oh!" She made a grab for the blanket and missed. His heat called to her even though he didn't move a muscle. The look on his face said all she needed to know. Heart-stopping. Smoldering. Intrigue.

Her brain yelled at her to go to him, to cling to his warmth, to never let go. With little room in her head devoted to rational thought, she closed her eyes and did the most natural thing she could think of—she shifted form and blew away.

Simon Foster watched the pixie of a woman dissipate into a wisp of opal smoke and take off into the night. In the time it took to blink an eye he lost sight of her in the darkness. With his luck, it had been a dream. After all, here he was in the middle of the night essentially stalking the woman his family insisted he could be fated to mate. The unfortunate thing in all this was that the woman he was in town to meet wasn't the redheaded Wind that had just made him smile for the first time all week.

Lighting one hand, he walked to the spot where the Wind had stood and plucked the discarded blanket from the ground. One good shake sent debris flying and the scent of vanilla and tea swirled around him in the night air. His heart pounded and a chill slithered up his spine; the foreign sensations registered in the back of his mind and pulled at strings he hadn't known were attached to his heart.

It had been at his parents' behest and his twin sister's impatient urging that he was in Harmony in the first place. Against his better judgment, he had taken time away from both his classroom and computer lab to be here and up until the Wind had arrived, he'd been having serious doubts. Tiffany Reese, aka the exploding blond, was the reason he'd come to the bar that night and lurked in the woods. But the little Wind 's arrival kept him rooted there. Goddess, he didn't need anything, especially a Wind, complicating what he hoped would be a straightforward trip. But his traitorous heart swelled at the memory of her materializing with nothing for cover but the afghan he now possessed. The image of her in the granny squared blanket was more enticing than seeing Tiffany bare-assed naked. Fate made a dream he hadn't known he dreamed come to fruition when the Wind lost her cover. Good Goddess, every bit of her creamy flesh had glistened in the moonlight.

Surprise rocked the foundation he stood on. Years of being called nerd, geek, and dork by beautiful women might be what had prejudiced him against Tiffany at first sight. Yet, the moment he had looked the gorgeous Wind in the eyes, he had lost track of his surroundings. She had knocked him for a curve—that was for sure. And poking fun at her had raised a pink spread of color on her cheeks that appealed to him in a way that he didn't dare think about. He shook her from his thoughts and threw the blanket over his shoulder.

His car was alongside the road about half a mile down and the night was getting colder with each passing minute. He stomped back into the trees and navigated the terrain with ease, thanks to the flickering flame in his hand. A wayward branch caught the scented material on his shoulder and pulled it into the darkness. He snatched it back, folded it with care, and tucked it safely under his arm. As ridiculous as it sounded to his own brain, he wanted to have it in his possession just in case he ran into the Wind again.

The problem with a small town was that a last minute trip meant he'd be rooming with his sister. Thankfully they'd been able to snag the last double room at the Belvidere B&B, so at least he'd have a bed to lay his head on instead of the floor.

The moment he turned the key in the lock, he knew he was in for a treat. The bedside clock read 3:57 a.m. and Siobhan was awake, upright in bed, a glare fixed on the door.

"Where have you been?"

"Out." He kicked off his boots and shrugged out of his coat before flopping on the bed closest to the door.

"Out where?" A light flicked on, bathing the

room in a harsh glow.

He laid an arm across his eyes to block the light and hide from the one woman who knew him well enough to do some actual damage. Being what humans would call 'supernatural,' wasn't the reason he and Siobhan were so close. Being twins was. Since birth, they had been able to feel out each other's mood. Of course, it was their dirty little secret. And by dirty little secret, he meant Siobhan oftentimes used it as a way to torment him.

"I went to the bar."

"But I thought you didn't want to go to the bar." A pillow hit him square in the chest. "I wanted you to come with me earlier when I went to schedule your date. Why go without me?"

He tucked the pillow under his head, keeping his eyes closed to the light and the pout he was sure Siobhan was sporting.

"Shiv, I needed to see what she was like before we got thrown into some silly date."

"Simon James Foster. Not every woman is like Cindy."

His sister's voice had quieted and he could feel the weight of her sympathy holding him fast to the bed like iron shackles.

"I know. I'm just not eager to be paraded around like some damn horse until Fate throws a woman my way."

The room darkened through his eyelids and the pillow was yanked out from under his resting head.

"You aren't being paraded around like a

stud, Si. Besides, I tried to tell you Cindy wasn't right for you. I could feel it, and so could you. You just chose to ignore it until she started spending your hard-earned cash."

His sister wasn't wrong. Cindy had pursued him relentlessly the entire time she'd been enrolled at the university and mocked him for following the no dating students rule. And it worked. On the evening of her graduation he had asked her out. He had hoped meeting his mate could be that simple. A shared love of technology, Chinese food, and sci-fi novels wasn't much to ask for, but when she practically moved in and asked to be put on his bank accounts, he knew something wasn't right. Lucky for him, he had his little sister there to rub his nose in it.

"I'm not the one hell-bent on finding me a mate, you know." He glared at his sister in the neon green light of the bedside clock.

"Well, you know what the books say better than I do," she waved her hand. "And you being older by seven minutes means I won't mate until after you do."

"That's not a fact. It's just the most common way it works." His rebuttal went unanswered. Sure, their dad was the community elder of Bohemia, New York, and they had grown up hearing all the ins and outs of the doctrines surrounding the Elemental community, but she was being ridiculous.

He felt the fight ebb from his sister's psyche before he heard her roll over to stare at the curtained windows. Silence made for easy company as his mind replayed the last few hours over and over and over again in all manners of fast forward, pause, and rewind possible.

From the other half of the room, his sister's breathing softened. He shucked his jeans and crawled under the covers. Visions of the Little Wind danced behind his closed eyes and lulled him to sleep. Images of her in the dark resurfaced. Something about the way the wind and moon had worked in tandem to create an ethereal image of her haunted him. He thought the encounter through again with hindsight as his measuring stick and knew, given the chance, he would do it all over again just to have those brief moments with her.

After a third go-around in his mind he was stunned to find that he had read her like a book. His gift had seen right through what he now could see had been false bravado. Funny though, his gift didn't give him insight into people like that. It preferred to work with unemotional things like computers, coding, and gadgets. With those things he could see how they worked and fit together most efficiently. But his Little Wind, she must've gotten to him at a level he wasn't used to, because looking back on it, he knew somewhere in the pit of his stomach that he had to speak to her the moment she had stomped her foot. A smile crept across his face as he recalled the way her chin had raised in defiance against his bad attempt at humor. Only moments later to have the air nearly knocked from his lungs completely by the musical sound of her laughter.

He'd been teasing when he'd claimed he'd give his right fireball to let her stoke his flame, but with every passing second, his body disagreed. Shaken to his core, he rolled onto his back and stared at the ceiling. In twenty-eight years, he never considered breaking an Elemental covenant. Not for fun. Not out of curiosity. Not for anything. Not until now.

Good Goddess, a little Wind was going to be his undoing.

4.

A car is only as reliable as the person who serviced it last. - Random Thought # 83

～

Elms pounded on the steering wheel of her ancient Jeep and mentally begged it to start, but nothing happened. It figured. She was running on fumes—mentally that was. Her Jeep boasted a full tank for all the good that did her. She was late for class, had to cancel on Tiffy, and was already flustered, thanks to the heated dreams that plagued her the last few hours. What was her problem? A stranger barely touched her and she was ready to what? Get burned alive? That's how it had felt when she fled. Like she had been willing to burn for him. How crazy was that? She closed her eyes and was assaulted once more with images of the tall, fiery stranger.

Ugh. Why was she wasting her time even thinking about him? Never in a hundred lifetimes would she stand a chance with him, no matter how heated her dreams had been. It was forbidden, and doing forbidden things never ended well. What was wrong with her? Fantasizing about a guy who was here strictly to meet someone else was insane. The realization made her heart sink.

A fat tear rolled over her lashes and landed with a soft thud in her lap. Nothing about this morning was going her way. Her heart wanted a guy she couldn't have, unless he was the last man on Earth, and her darn car was intent on giving her a heart attack with its sputtering engine that quit at the most inopportune times, for example, the blind curve along the mountainous riverside where she now sat. She banged her fists on the steering wheel as more tears fled in a torrent.

At least now that the sun was up, the likelihood of her getting hit by another car had diminished. She had already placed a call to her friend and novice mechanic, Colin, but he wasn't answering his cell. Crappity, crap, crap. Maybe her cousin would be able to at least pick her up. Before her fingers finished flying over the buttons to place the call, a tapping on the passenger window sent her pulse into overdrive. She looked up and met blue eyes that were more familiar than they should have been.

"Are you okay? I didn't mean to startle y..."

His voice trailed off and a look akin to disbelief crossed his face. "It's you—from last night. I'd recognize that hair anywhere."

Just her luck to be stranded and have the first person to find her be the guy she'd let burn her alive. Happily.

"Oh, I'm okay," she yelled through the closed window. "I'm just waiting for my cousin. He should be here any minute." She hoped the lie would send him on his merry way.

"I can wait with you until he comes. Better yet, I could look under the hood for you."

"No need. Declan'll be here soon to give me a ride and I'll get it towed. There's no reason for you to be late to wherever you're headed." Her words rambled together in one nervous string of word vomit while her heart skipped a beat.

"It's no problem. Pop the hood and let me make a quick call." He hooked his thumb over his shoulder at a sleek black sedan idling on the shoulder of the road.

"Okay," she surrendered. His persistence was flattering. She nodded and fumbled for her cell phone in the cup holder. While Fire Guy ran to his car, she hit call and waited while the ringer droned in her ear. When Declan's voicemail answered, she left a curt message. "When you get this, there's a small chance I'll be dead—burned alive by a Fire Starter here to woo Tiffy. But if you get this in the next few seconds, could you please get your butt in the car and come rescue me? I'm stranded on River Road about two miles downstream of Charlie's place. Thanks—I hope."

She stabbed the disconnect button and sent a silent prayer into the ether that Declan would find her body quickly if things went bad. Jolted from her thoughts, Fire Guy was back standing at her door with a silly grin pasted to his face.

"Pop the hood," he repeated. "I'll take a look and see if we can get you going."

She fumbled for the hood lever and wracked her brain for a reason to stay in the safety of her car. Something about having the glass and metal separating them gave her the courage to believe she wasn't a moth headed directly for a flame. Another tap sounded on her window, dumping more adrenaline into her bloodstream.

"When I say so, try turning it over."

"Okay," she called through the closed window.

"You know, it'd be easier to hear each other if you'd put the window down."

"Oh, that's okay. It's pretty cold out today and I didn't bring my coat." It sounded reasonable. She just hoped he didn't look in the backseat where her heavy parka rested.

"Whatever you want Little Wind."

"That's not my name, you know." She regretted the words the minute they left her lips.

"Understood. You didn't give me your name last night. My mother taught me better than to call a woman 'hey you'." He smiled and ducked his head back under the hood of her Jeep. "Try starting it now," he yelled.

She whispered a prayer to the Goddess of motor vehicles and turned the key. It resulted in the same empty clicking sound as before. Drat. Her cell phone rattled in the cup holder. Saved by the text message. She read the screen and deflated. It was Declan. He was already in New York for the day, but he offered to call Colin to see if he could come to her rescue in his absence. Before she could tap out a reply, Fire Guy was back at the window.

"I think your alternator might be bad. It shouldn't be hard to replace, but you're stuck until your ride arrives."

"About that," she held up the cell, "he can't make it after all."

"I could give you a ride." He shrugged and offered her a smile.

"My momma taught me to never get in a car with a stranger. And as you said earlier, I don't even know your name, Fire Guy."

He burst out laughing. "Fire Guy. Ha. That's hilarious, Little Wind. But, to appease your dear mother, let me introduce myself. Simon Foster. I'm from Long Island and I teach tech classes at the local university." He smiled and gestured at her through the window to reciprocate.

"While I'm sure it'd be a pleasure to meet you, I'm still not getting in your car." She gave a little smile and sent a text back to Declan. *Yes, call Colin now, please!* When her phone buzzed in her hand the readout had a single word, *Done*.

"And I'm sure my new ride will be here at any moment." She shivered. She longed to reach back and grab her coat, but she didn't want to get caught in her ever-increasing web of lies and misconceptions.

"Little Wind, you're cold. If you don't want me to drive you anywhere, at least let me in to warm you up."

When she said nothing, he ducked beneath the hood, unclipped something, and let the hood shut with a solid thunk.

"Okay, I'll just stand here and wait until you either get too cold or your ride arrives."

"I'll be fine. You don't need to stay," she insisted while rubbing her hands together to combat the cold that seeped into her bones.

"You say that now, but if your friend doesn't show up and you die of exposure, how would I live with myself?"

His eyebrow rose with the question but she couldn't detect anything smug in his words.

Simon watched a multitude of emotions wash over the redhead's face. He stepped back from the car, raised his hands in the air in surrender, and bowed low enough so she could still see his face when he spoke.

"I promise I'm not crazy or anything. I know last night was awkward…"

"I'm pretty sure you meant to say creepy," she cut in, yelling through the window.

"Okay. Creepy. But I have references. I can

call my sister; she'll vouch for me."

"Hmmm, I don't doubt you'd come with references, Fire Guy."

"Simon. Call me Simon."

Before she answered, she held up the index finger of her left hand and wrestled a cell phone from a cup holder with her right.

"Colin." Her tone relaxed, as did her posture.

Whoever this Colin was, she appeared happy to hear from him. With his luck, Colin was her boyfriend. Simon derailed that train of thought as soon as it ran through his head. What did it matter if she had a boyfriend? It wasn't like he had any claim on her. He dropped his hands and studied her while he waited for their conversation to finish. His knack for seeing the beauty of things that matched in perfect harmony buzzed in his subconscious again.

It was odd, when this Wind had an emotion shift, he was aware of it in a way he never experienced with anyone other than Siobhan. And at this very moment, he saw distress in her aura as she dropped the phone from her ear. Before he could ask why she was upset, his cell phone chirped in his pocket. He pulled it from its denim confines and sighed when he read the digital read-out.

"What?" He growled as he answered his phone.

"Where are you? I'm at the Americana with Tiffany. We've been here waiting for you." His sister huffed on the other end of the connection.

"Oh shit. What time is it?"

"It's already after eleven, Si. Get your ass here and quick! If Mom hears that you screwed up your first meeting with your mate, she'll be pissed."

"I don't think she's my mate, Shiv."

"Look, I knew you snuck out to meet her last night. I woke up when the connection started to form, that's why I was up waiting for you. You know that's how this twin thing works. I can tell your souls have connected. This morning when I saw her, I could feel the connection. Don't leave your mate hanging. For the love of the Goddess, drop whatever you are doing and get your ass here pronto!"

A lump formed in the back of his throat and he struggled to find words. It couldn't be. He couldn't possibly be fated for the hot head with no control over her abilities. He made a noncommittal sound, disconnected, and pocketed the phone. Shit. He was sunk if Shiv was right. But, from the moment he had seen the Wind behind the wheel of the broken down Jeep, a reel of possibilities had danced through his brain.

Siobhan had to be mistaken. His future couldn't be tied to a woman so explosive when a girl so airy and light created a hunger within like he'd never before experienced. His shoulders drooped. Damn Fate for being so cruel. He just wanted a quiet life with a woman who made him feel like he felt right here right now. Dread spread from the pit of his stomach to the far reaches of his being. Shit. What was wrong with him? His head pounded and nausea reared its ugly head from the bottom of his gut. The sound of a door shutting brought his attention back to the present.

"Are you all right? You don't look so good."

His Little Wind stood before him, concern reflected in the bluest eyes he had ever seen. Goddess, those eyes were as deep as the ocean and he eagerly took the plunge, falling into their depths without a second thought. This is what he'd always thought meeting his mate would feel like—not whatever it was his sister had droned on about.

"I'm not sure. I mean, I'll be fine," he said with a stutter as he looked for an escape.

"Are you sure? I train with the local healer, so if there's something I can do to help..." She trailed off, leaving words unsaid, but he watched as her aura swirled around her in vibrant hues until it settled in a clear red that licked at her like flames. Seeing her like that awakened a piece of his soul he had never known existed and called to his very essence.

That was about the time the world tilted a little too far to the left and his vision darkened.

5.

When all else fails, panic. Wait, that can't be right... -
Random Thought # 269

∿

The blue of Simon's eyes faded to deep grey then pitch black like the fire within him had died. Bile rose in Elms' throat. Not again. Could she maintain another Fire's well-being without tossing her cookies? Oh Goddess, she hoped so. Simon cantered to the right, unsteady and leaned heavily on the hood of her Jeep.

Oh no. He was going down despite his insistence to the contrary. She judged him to outweigh her by a solid hundred pounds, which meant any attempt to catch him would only be an exercise in humiliating futility. The notion of being crushed by the Fire blinked in and out of her brain when the hip hop ringer of her cell butted in.

Indecision warred in her head. There wasn't a useful thought making its way through her misfiring synapses except that maybe the person on the other end of the call would be better suited to fix whatever was happening to Simon. His head lolled to the side and his face paled. Crap on a stick. She sized him up again for good measure and called to the wind. Adding a bit of her own wind essence to the welcome gust, she managed to get him safely to the semi-frozen ground.

She laid a hand on his forehead and was overwhelmed by the temperature of his skin. The pulse point in his neck raced under her cold fingers, while the color drained from his lips.

"Simon? Can you hear me?" She knelt down and shook his shoulder. No response. Doubt crept in and struggled with her better senses until she shoved it all deep down into the pit of her being and rushed to grab her medical kit from the back of her car. The bag bounced and toppled when she dropped it to the ground beside her unwitting patient. She riffled through the pack and pulled out the tiny bottle of blue crystals labeled "Awake." Nothing more than a herbal concoction that worked well for headaches and fainting, she uncorked the vial and waved it beneath his nose.

His lashes fluttered and his lids sprang open as the herbal mixture tickled his senses. Color returned to his face and a quick check of his pulse reassured her that he was coming around. She used the moment to take in the slight crook of his nose. Hmm, a healed broken nose. It didn't fit the image he had portrayed of being a college professor, but neither did the Doc Marten boots he wore, or that slick car that was idling behind them—that slick car with a grill ornament that resembled the Devil's pitchfork. Pretty sure a college professor couldn't afford one of those. Simon Foster was one big contradiction after another.

He sputtered labored breaths while his eyes went wide and stared at her face. She focused her attention to his aura and found a muddy blue color that explained the labored breathing.

"Don't panic. It will only make it worse," she chided. She unfastened his coat and slid a hand over the broad expanse of his chest to feel the telltale beating of his heart. She sat in complete silence and focused on the rapid staccato that played beneath his ribs. Closing her eyes, she added a second hand to his chest and began to hum an old lullaby while tracing the notes with tiny strokes of her fingers. Just as she'd hoped, his heart began to slow and match the tempo of her caress.

Her breath caught in her throat when his hand slid over hers and stilled them on his chest. Did she dare meet his eyes? She swallowed her fear and turned a cautious gaze his way.

"I'm not sure what you just did, but thank you."

His voice was low and coated in velvet. His eyes returned to cobalt and his aura was now a crisp yellow. She stared a moment too long and was rewarded with a rush of heat that shot up her arm from their point of contact. A flash of color stained his aura a brilliant shade of burnt-orange. She shook her head and pulled from his grasp. She had no business looking at him with her gifts. He wasn't her client and hadn't asked her to look inside, so she was essentially eavesdropping on his emotional state. But, she couldn't keep the blush that stained her cheeks away. She'd seen the burnt-orange aura many times before—mostly at The Outpost when lovers became intent on finding a quiet corner to indulge in some quality 'alone time.'

She sat back on her heels, repacked her kit, and vowed to never touch Simon again. She tossed the bag's strap over her shoulder and stood.

"It was nothing. How are you feeling now?"

"Better. Bad news and low blood sugar aren't a good breakfast choice." He shook his head.

"Are you diabetic? I might have some glucose tablets in here somewhere," she offered, pawing through her bag.

"Not diabetic. Hypoglycemic. I have a drink in my car."

He struggled to get up, but gravity wasn't working with him. He slumped against Elms and her legs buckled beneath her. She grabbed him around the waist and leaned against her car until he was able to hold his weight.

"Let me get that drink for you."

She dropped her bag on the ground, jogged to his car, opened the door, and was assaulted with the smell of leather conditioner and sandalwood. The front cup holders housed change and other miscellaneous things. She climbed into the rich red leather seat and looked in the back. There in the cup holder was a bottle of orange juice. Perfect. She grabbed it and climbed out of the car. Simon looked almost normal leaning against her uncooperative Jeep. The dark wash jeans, leather jacket, white Henley, and black Docs made quite the picture.

She cracked open the juice and handed him the open bottle.

"Drink up."

"Thanks." He took a long gulp of the juice then pierced her with a stare. "You know, you still haven't told me your name. It's hard to thank someone without a name."

"Oh." She considered giving him a fake name, but she was already in too deep with the lies. "Elms. My name is Elms," she mumbled.

"That's a big name for such a tiny creature." He took a slow swig of the juice, but his eyes never wandered from her body.

The noise of an approaching vehicle grabbed her attention. The engine slowed as it entered the curve leading to the stretch of the road where they were parked. A familiar jacked-up pickup swerved across the road and pulled to a stop almost nose to nose with her Jeep. Colin jumped out and rounded the truck faster than she could track with her eyes.

"El. You 'kay?"

His voice rumbled on a growl that sounded like it was ripped straight from his core. She swore she caught a glimpse of a snarl directed at Simon when he shrugged out of his thick flannel coat and wrapped her in it's warmth. He gave her an awkward side hug of sorts and put himself between her and the perceived threat that was Simon. The gesture was both possessive and reassuring all at once.

"Colin, meet Simon Foster. He's here to court Tiffy." She gestured in Simon's direction. "He happened to find me this morning."

"Sure he did." The doubt in Colin's voice rang clear. "What'd ya do to him? He doesn't look so good." Colin leaned close and lowered his voice for her ears only. "Did he pull somethin'? If he did, say the word and I'll kick his ass." His grey eyes darkened to slate; black and ominous.

"It wasn't anything like that, I swear. He was fine one minute, and the next, he looked like someone had stolen the life right out of him. Turned out to be low blood sugar—nothing I couldn't handle."

"Whatever you say, Doc. How about we send him on his way and I get you home?" Colin's deliberate words landed as effectively as a slap to her face. "I'm sure your aunt and uncle are worried about you."

"Uh…" What was he talking about? Her aunt and uncle knew she wouldn't be home until later. She chanced a look at Simon from the corner of her eye and the heat returned to her face. His heartbeat echoed across the few feet that separated them and joined hers.

"It was nice to meet you, Elms." He cocked his head to the side, "I'll be on my way. My sister is expecting me." Simon smiled and turned toward his car.

"Nice to meet you, too," she called after him. Colin bent to snag her emergency bag then wrapped a protective arm around her shoulders.

"Is there anything you need outta this old heap of junk?" Colin asked, steering her away from Simon's retreating figure.

"What?" She tried to focus on Colin's words, but the warmth that had simmered somewhere deep inside faded with each of Simon's footsteps. The loss of his warmth sent a bone-rattling chill through her entire being.

Compelled by unknown forces, she turned as he raised a hand in salute and drove away. She wouldn't swear to it, but his aura dissolved into muddy green when he saw Colin's arm still around her shoulder.

6.

Can someone please tell me where the music is? I hear it's time to face it... - Random Thought # 740

~ひ

It was almost noon when Simon pulled into the parking lot of the Americana Diner. He parked next to Siobhan's sporty SUV and sat for a moment gathering his thoughts. The drive to the diner only took a few minutes, but something had weighed heavy on his heart the entire way. He'd called Siobhan to let her know that he had been detained, but that he wasn't canceling. When they had spoken, he could feel a pull that seemed to be driving him closer to something. It was too bad he couldn't shake the feeling that he was on his way to meet his executioner rather than his life-mate.

He saw his twin step out onto the Diner's porch and wave in his direction. He knew her well enough to know that she wasn't waving hello. Nope, she was telling him to get his ass out of the car. Pronto. He took a deep breath and pulled himself to his feet.

The Americana was a typical New Jersey diner complete with a mouthy waitress that hollered a generic welcome as he followed his sister in. But before he could lay eyes on Tiffany, Siobhan grabbed his arm and stopped him by the cashier's station.

"What took you so long? You do remember that we were supposed to meet Tiffany at eleven, right?" She kept her voice low, but he could hear the notes of barely concealed anger. "And you look like shit. Did you forget to eat breakfast again?"

"I know. I took a drive to clear my head and found someone stranded on the side of the road. I waited until her ride came along." He figured the less he divulged about his encounter with Elms, the better when it came to his sister. It was bad enough that if he was to ever run into Elms with his sister, Siobhan would know instantaneously that he found Elms intriguing. "I had some orange juice."

"You need to eat something. There's something called disco fries on the table. They look gross, but taste delicious. Eat them."

"You know I am a grown-ass man, right? I can take care of myself."

"Ri-i-i-ight. That's why you're late. And

your sugar is low." Siobhan shook her head. "The only reason Tiffy's still here is because I ratted you out and told her the weird feelings she was experiencing had to be the start of the bonding process."

"Huh?" He took a beat to suss out the emotions running through him at the moment. While he felt some new tingles and flashes of interest, it didn't compare to the building heat that he'd felt when he looked at Elms. The thought of those endless blue pools Elms called eyes made his heart skip a beat.

"See, Si. I told you that you were bonding. I'll go sit at the counter and you go talk to her yourself. I don't want to get in the way." Her smile was so big, he could practically see her darn molars before she skipped off to the stools at the counter.

He ran a hand through his hair and tried to find the courage to make himself turn and walk right out the door he had come in, but it wasn't in him. He couldn't stand up this woman his sister thought he was fated to be with—even if the idea of her made gooseflesh rise on his skin in the chilled-to-the-bone sense.

He turned into the main dining room and found Tiffy without any problem. She sat perched at the edge of a red plastic-covered cushioned bench in a booth by the back bank of windows. From her vantage point, she had probably seen him sitting in his car debating whether to come in or not, but at least she wouldn't have been able to see Shiv giving him crap in the vestibule.

Tiffy's long blond hair was pulled back into a neat ponytail and the delicate slope of her neck intrigued him. It was the first time he'd ever noticed such a thing on a woman. He rounded the booth and stopped beside her. In the broad daylight he saw what he completely missed last night—she was beautiful. Not a lick of makeup touched her face, her lashes were thick, her cheekbones high, and her mouth heart-shaped.

"Sorry I'm late. I'm Simon." He extended his hand in her direction but she didn't take it. After a few beats, he dropped it to his side. "May I join you?"

She studied him carefully before she responded, "I know I'm supposed to just say 'yes, have a seat,' but I'll be honest with ya—I'm annoyed as hell that you're so late. You're damn lucky Siobhan is so generous with her time. And of course, it helps that you're not half bad looking, but I guess that runs in the family."

"Thanks, I guess." He slid into the booth opposite Tiffany. "I didn't plan on being late. I swear. It was more of a situation of circumstance."

"Just like you spying on me last night? Was that a situation of circumstance as well?"

He smiled. She was feisty. He'd never imagined his mate, but someone who could challenge him a bit might not be such a bad thing. "Touché. I guess I wanted to know what I was getting into. Is that creepy? A little bird told me that it was creepy." He trailed off when he looked up and saw something he never expected to see—

Elms—and she was walking in their direction. His heart jumped. She seemed oblivious to his presence, but it struck him that he intuitively knew she was worried. He took a closer look at the aura coming off her and was surprised to find it a dim grey with a concentrated area of blackness near her left breast. That couldn't be right. The woman had seemed so light and airy earlier. Almost fairy-like, but this version of her was guarded, and extremely well around her heart, if that dark spot was any indicator. If that guy, Colin, had done something to hurt her, Goddess help him because Simon was going to beat the living shit out of him for hurting such a precious woman.

"Definitely creepy, but I'm sure I can forgive you, especially considering all the nice things your sister had to say about you. Plus I understand you and Siobhan are a package deal. Simon, are you even listening to me?"

He pulled his eyes from Elms for a brief instant.

"I'm sorry. What were you saying?" No matter how hard he tried, he couldn't keep himself from watching Elms make her way to an empty corner booth. She spilled an armload of books onto the table in a pile of bound paper chaos. When the waitress stopped by Elms' table, she poured steaming water into the mug and added a tea bag like this was a standing appointment.

"You have got to be kidding me. Your sister said you have a hard time staying focused on the here and now, but this is just rude. There is no way in hell that I am going to spend forever with a man who can't even hold a five-minute conversation without his mind wandering off into the abyss, no matter how lovely his sister is. I'm outta here. When you're ready to actually settle down, have Siobhan call me."

Simon was barely aware of Tiffany's outrage. He was consumed by Elms. Nothing Tiffy said registered in his mind, let alone the fact that she was currently stomping her long legs right out the door.

"What did you do?"

Siobhan's voice broke his concentration. Where had she come from? Simon jerked his attention from Elms long enough to see his sister seated in the booth across from him.

"Tiffy just ran out of here like she was shot from a freaking cannon. What did you do?"

"Nothing. I think. I mean, I don't think I did anything," he hedged.

"Of course you didn't do anything. You got distracted again, didn't you? Look, even though you are fated to be with Tiffy, you can't go around treating her like you do everyone else who interrupts that big brain of yours."

Thank the Goddess that his sister's gift was the typical Fire gift of slipping into a flammable gelatinous state, because if she had the gift of death rays that shot from her eyes or something, he'd be belly up dead at this very moment.

"I'll make it up to her." He had the good sense to look contrite when he made the promise.

His twin had the uncanny ability to see right through him, if she so desired, and he really wasn't up for one of her temper tantrums. He was too preoccupied with whatever it was that made Elms' aura so dark and bleak.

"I'll go find her and see if we can reschedule. I'll tell her you're hung over or something. It'll give you time to get your act together so you don't blow the one good thing that is about to happen to you, big brother." With a flourish she was off.

He watched his sister's brisk retreat to the door and was reminded of their mother. It had never occurred to him until this moment that he and his twin were polar opposites. Where he was dark, she was light. He had a slight build that he could fill out when challenged, but she was soft and round. Her hair was almost platinum blond where his was dark, her eyes were the color of melted chocolate where his were bluer than the ocean midday. It was as if their spots of light contradicted each other's darkness. In all their years on this planet it had never bothered them that they were so different in appearance because they were so similar in so many other ways. Which made her rebuke sting even more. Siobhan was right. He needed to learn to focus on the people who loved him, because his disinterest was a huge put-off. And Siobhan was talking from experience.

A little over a year ago she had met a nice human guy who she thought might be a good placeholder until she met her fated mate, but as all things Foster twins went, she blew it up. She became obsessed with the lack of complete connection with him and went a little crazy. She tried to fabricate a connection that could mimic the Elemental bonding process to the point of scaring him away. That was when she began hunting every corner of the globe for her mate and, subsequently, his. Because it wouldn't be enough for her to find her Mister Right. No. She had it in her mind that they would find their ideal mates together, and as with all the major milestones in their lives, they would marry their mates together in what he envisioned to be the most fucked up double wedding of all time.

The thud of a book hitting the floor drew him from his thoughts. This was his moment. Something deep down inside rallied and he was across the room in a flash. By the time Elms was bending to retrieve the fallen book, he was already there on bended knee with the book in his hands. He watched with rapt attention as her aura changed when her eyes lit with recognition. The dark spot near her heart stayed intact, but the rest of the greyness faded to a clear red.

Interesting. Maybe he was reading her all wrong, but in his limited experience with women who found him attractive, this was the color he associated with their response to him. A smile pulled at the corner of his mouth. He drew himself up to his full height, all six feet and that extra inch, and he made sure to stand as close as he could to her while he flipped over the text.

"Mating Rituals of Fire Elementals. Wow, talk about some hot reading, Little Wind. What would inspire a sweet little thing like you to be curious about the mating rituals of Fires?"

"Ohmygoddess. What are you doing here?"

The words rushed from her mouth on a wave of vanilla and tea, assaulting him with warmth, and wrapped around his soul. Simon couldn't help himself. He had to be near her. He nudged her over with his leg and slid into the booth beside her until she couldn't move any further, and their sides were almost pressed together.

"If you want to know about the mating rituals of Fires, just ask. I'm an open book." He slid the actual book in question to the far edge of the table and scooted even closer, relishing every lick of heat that met him where their bodies connected. Now this is what being mated should feel like. He chanced a look down into her angelic face and was met with those eyes that sucked him in.

"Are you following me?" She quirked her head to the side and looked him up and down. "I can't figure you out. There's something going on, but I can't for the life of me put my finger on what it is about you. I hope you aren't planning on hurting Tiffy. She's been through so much recently. I'm not sure she could recover from..."

She paused and he held his breath, waiting to see how she'd choose to finish her thought.

She didn't disappoint. "I'm not sure she could recover from falling for you and losing you."

With that simple admission, the spot of

color over her heart turned muddy green. That's when it all became clear. His Little Wind was jealous of Tiffy.

7.

Sometimes the world seems a lot smaller than everyone says it is. - Random Thought # 923

∽

Elms regretted the words the moment they left her mouth. She wished she could bend time and just reel them back in. To make matters worse, the smile on Simon's face was dangerously ensnaring.

"Look Elms, I know we've just met, but I'm serious about helping you. Scout's honor." He held up his first three fingers and touched his thumb to his pinky. The look of sincerity was genuine, but she detected a trace of mischief in the small smile he was barely able to conceal.

"Is that the hand sign for the girl scouts?"

She laughed at the realization. Here was this grown man, sitting so close that she swore she could feel his pulse through the leg of her jeans where their legs touched, and he was flashing her the girl scout sign while promising to help her get her client mated and safely out of the fire.

"Oh shit. I honestly don't know." He looked confused for a moment before he burst out laughing. "My sister, Siobhan, was a girl scout. That must be where I picked it up. You know, no one's ever mentioned it before."

His chuckle erupted into a full-blown belly laugh that drew her in all on its own accord.

"So I take it you never were a boy scout?" She couldn't contain the matching laughter in her voice.

He shook his head and wrinkled his nose. She met his eyes while she waited for him to catch his breath and answer her. His eyes were the most curious mixture of blues that she had ever seen before. Blue wasn't enough of a description for the color that drew her in. The depth of them reminded her of an endless void that she was falling into. Twisting. Turning. Tumbling with him until she and he no longer existed as individuals, instead were a unique mixture of them both that was as delicate as a precious gemstone.

No, blue was not enough of a description when it came to his eyes. The very edge of color was a warm golden band that glowed and brightened with each laugh and smile that crossed his lips, and it led to a deeper blue. One that reminded her of the middle of the ocean; a place where sirens called and sailors got lost for all time. In that instant it occurred to her that if she ever had the choice to choose eyes to stare into for the rest of her earthly life, his would be the ones she'd beg, borrow, and steal to have—even if it meant losing herself in the process.

Abigail, the Americana's veteran waitress extraordinaire, stopped by the table at that precise moment to refill her tea. She was known for her perceptiveness almost as much as her ability to share gossip and that was the last thing Elms needed.

"I didn't know you were expecting company this morning, Elma," Abigail intoned, as her eyebrows rose so high Elms swore they would get lost in her coiffed, straight-from-a-bottle red hair.

Her given name took her by surprise. It was the only time she could remember the waitress using it in all her times frequenting the diner.

"Oh, this is an old friend of mine from back home," Elms said, without meeting the older woman's eyes. "Do you still take your tea with cream and sugar?" Elms directed the question to Simon and hoped he could read the desperate plea in her eyes.

"Actually, I do." Elms let loose a sigh of relief when he turned his handsome smile Abigail's way. "And if it isn't too much trouble, could I get it in a to-go cup? Oh, and one for my friend as well. She promised me a tour of Harmony, and well, a tour in the winter is always better when you have something to warm you from the inside."

A rush of pink flooded Abigail's face and Elms could only imagine that Simon had actually had the nerve to wink at the woman. What was he thinking? He would ruin her reputation with nonsense like that.

"You New Yorkers and your take-out beverages…" The waitress shook her head and graced them with a sufficiently chastised look. "Well, just give me a minute and I'll have you ready to go in no time." She pasted on a smile and practically skipped from the table, which was amazing considering she had to be at least in her mid-fifties.

Yeah, the whole town was soon going to hear about the man who wanted to warm her from the inside out. This situation was fast becoming a disaster and, in times like these, Elms didn't have a single point of reference for who to call.

As soon as Abigail disappeared from the dining room, Elms leaned into Simon to hiss a reprimand in his ear, but a flash of heat licked her from head to toe with the contact. She jumped away, shocked by the sensation.

"What was that?"

To his credit, Simon had the decency to look equally surprised by the heat that had overcome him. Without saying a word, he gently reached across her and began closing the books she had open all over the table and placed them in a neat pile. When only Mating Rituals of Elementals was left to stack, he pulled it close, flipped it open to a section near the beginning of the book, then slid it in front of Elms, all without a word.

She looked at the open book before her and skimmed the first page until she saw a passage that nearly jumped out at her and punched her in the nose.

When a male Fire Elemental becomes aroused, he may become overheated. In this case, one should be careful with spontaneous bodily contact so to not become burned.

"Oh." The word slipped from between her lips on a breath as she closed the book and moved it to the top of the stack. She couldn't make herself meet his eyes; those magical eyes that she craved. Nope. There was no coming back from what she just read.

A lump formed in the back of her throat and she let it sit there. What did you say to someone once you realized they were attracted to you? In her slightly over twenty-one years on this planet, it had never been something she worried about. Maybe it was because she knew until she met her destined mate, there was no reason to waste time thinking about things like what to say to a man who expressed interest in her. Especially not a man who had the potential to burn her alive in all senses of the phrase.

What concerned her the most was that being burned alive by Simon didn't sound as scary as it should.

She could feel the weight of his stare on her face, but she refused to meet it. Instead, she focused on the teacup sitting in front of her and wished with all her might that there was a way to disentangle the strands of conflicting emotions and basic incompatibilities. If that could be accomplished, then maybe she might find a way to be brave enough to touch him again—just to see what would happen next.

Abigail chose that moment to deliver the to go teas. She slipped a bill on the table and walked away without uttering a thing, which only added to the tension radiating between them. Elms sat transfixed, afraid to move, fearful the repercussions from a slight brush of her arm against his would send her up in flames, but also intrigued. Simon shifted beside her, brushing his arm against her shoulder, and tiny licks of flame danced along her entire side. She chanced a glance at him from the corner of her eye and was stunned to see him watching her with careful interest as he pulled his wallet from his rear pocket.

"Let's get out of here." His voice slid like silk over her nerve endings. "I don't know what's happening between us, but if I don't touch you again, I *will* lose my mind."

She knew she should say no and let him go, but every nerve ending was dancing, craving his warmth almost like she had been frozen her entire life and he had just started to melt her. It was addicting. She wanted to throw caution to the wind and see what would happen if she did add her wind to his fire like he had teased last night.

The possibilities rolled through her mind.

She wanted to leap to his side and rush out the door with him hand in hand. But the practical voice that lived in her head shouted that it would be a terrible mistake. He was one of Tiffy's suitors, and she wouldn't be helping Tiffy if she started getting cozy with her prospective mates. And from what Tiffy had said last night, Simon was by far the best suitor in town.

She couldn't betray Tiffy like that no matter what her heart wanted. Elms focused on the jukebox in the corner of the diner and exhaled. It was the right thing. The only thing. Decision made. Now only the difficult task of forcing the lump in her throat away remained. Then she'd be able to find the words to send him on his merry way. Or at the very least, she'd wait him out. He was bound to get bored of staring at her soon.

She struggled with that darn lump. It felt like concrete in her trachea. Then Simon did the one thing that could undo her resolve; he slid his hand into her hair, angled her head, and brushed his lips across hers. If that wasn't temptation enough, the heat that spread straight from the spot where their lips met to every square inch of her body was.

"I shouldn't. You're here to meet Tiffy," she whispered when he moved his lips a fraction of an inch from hers.

"I met Tiffy. You are far more interesting, Little Wind." He rested his forehead gently on hers. "I'll ask you once more to leave with me. You can say no, but I need you to know I'm hoping you'll say yes."

The inner debate that had been in favor of saying no moments ago was quieted. Her pulse drummed a rapid staccato through her veins.

"Say it. Say yes."

The gold rims of his eyes blazed.

She took a deep breath and jumped in. "Yes."

8.

Up in flames has just taken on a whole new meaning.
- Random Thought #376

∽᷍

Elms didn't remember leaving the diner and sliding into his sleek car. The heat in the car was stifling. Add to the heat the pounding base of some alternative band she'd never heard before, and she was slowly losing the ability to think. She spun the dial on the dash to its coldest setting, even though remnants of last week's snow still covered the ground. When that didn't quell the heat, she mashed the button for the window until fresh mountain air whipped her face and sent her wild hair flying.

"Are you hot or scared?"

He was too perceptive. Too bad it didn't irk her enough to make her demand that he turn the car around and return her to the safety of the diner and her research.

"Does it matter?" She knew it didn't. He already knew what it was.

"That's what I thought." He gave her his half smile and slid his window down to match hers. The wind rushing through the car tussled his hair, sending it upright in every which way. "Where to, Little Wind?"

The question caught her off guard. "Uh, I thought you had someplace in mind." She watched trees race by as he steered around curves with ease.

"I've got an idea." He shifted the car into a lower gear and made a hairpin turn onto Ridge Road. The tires caught on residual deicing salt and shot them up the mountain until he slid them around another hairpin turn onto Swamp Road.

"Where are we going?" Her knuckles turned white from holding onto the dash. Speeding was going to get them killed, but every time he hit the brakes, the heat ratcheted up another degree. It was like he was trying to outrun an inferno that was hot on their heels.

"I'm pretty sure I saw a reservoir on the map around here somewhere."

"You know there's nothing there besides the reservoir and trees, right?"

"That's what I was banking on, Little Wind. Nothing but you, me, and a big body of water in case things get out of control."

Heat shot up her face. He couldn't be thinking what she thought he was.

"Simon…" She paused, afraid to break the spell being woven between them.

"Don't worry, Elms. I'm almost positive we won't burn anything to the ground." He smiled at her before turning his eyes back to the road.

Unable to stitch together a witty retort, she stared open-mouthed as they turned onto a secluded area off the side of the road. She could see the water through the trees. The heat in the car was building again to the likes of a first-alarm fire. The second he shifted the car into park, she bolted from the vehicle and tried to put some distance between them.

" Good grief, is that heat all you?" she called over her shoulder as she darted into the wooded tree line. The sound of his heavy footsteps on the old snow and dead leaves was her only answer. When she hit a clearing near the reservoir, she skidded to a stop and took a lungful of fresh crisp air in to soothe the fire that was burning inside her.

Simon's heavy footsteps neared and then his arms, strong and sure, wrapped around her, pressing her into him, searing them together. Fire licked at every point of contact and singed her to the bone. She yelped and he reluctantly released her putting a few feet of safe distance between them.

She saw under his arm the afghan that she had lost the previous night at The Outpost. He set it down on the ground and stalked closer to her.

Slowly this time.

"I don't know what it is about you, Elms, but I can't make myself stay away. I just need to touch you. It's the only thing that makes the burning inside me stop." He moved ever closer and she retreated, matching him step for step.

This wasn't a man ready to teach her about Fires. This was a man who would teach her about passion. Red, hot, steamy passion. And even though it was a lesson she wanted to learn, she knew she shouldn't. Not here. Not now. Not with him.

"Simon, you know as well as I do that even if we do what you are suggesting..." She trailed off and he stopped moving, waiting. "...Well, it won't be able to mean anything. You understand, right?"

Simon studied the tiny pixie of a woman before him and wondered what he was thinking. He knew Siobhan said it was Tiffy he was supposed to be with, but every second he spent with Elms made him question everything he knew about the bonding process. How was it possible to be fated to one woman when another was the only person who made him burn like this?

He watched the winter wind caress her pale skin and toss her hair into a red tornado of color bronzed by the winter sun. In this moment it didn't matter if Tiffy was his mate, because if he turned and walked away from Elms right now, he wasn't sure he could make himself be content with Tiffy for a lifetime.

He had to know what it would be like to be one with Elms. The erection he'd been trying to keep under wraps throbbed heavily in his jeans, while the overwhelming desire to kiss her consumed him. Braced for her refusal, he took the first slow steps in her direction. He was thrilled when she didn't make an effort to move away from him. Instead, she took a step forward.

"I can't make myself say no to you. Promise not to burn me alive?" she whispered in his ear as she slid her arms around his shoulders.

"I'll do my best."

He breathed in her scent and sealed it away in his soul.

The fire within danced higher and higher with every touch of her fingers on him. When she raised herself onto her toes and placed a tentative kiss on his chin, he nearly lost hold of his control. He leaned down to meet her kiss with one of his own, and when she parted her lips in silent invitation, the last semblance of sanity he clung to went up in smoke.

He felt the moment the fire within took over and began to consume him. A curl of smoke twirled around them as his clothes started to singe at the edges. When her tongue made a tentative exploration of his mouth, he pulled her tight against his chest. He closed his eyes and drifted on the feelings as they washed over him. It wasn't until Elms shoved against his chest that he realized the fire running through his veins had taken actual form and was burning every stitch of fabric off of him in this very cold, very open place.

"Simon!" Elms' yell pulled him into the present. "You're on fire." She grabbed for the afghan and swung on him, looking like she was ready to brave the flames to wrap him in it, but she stopped at the last moment.

Simon watched the panic on her face grow while his skin smoldered. Too bad that in times like these, he lost the ability to speak and all he could do was make a reassuring gesture to let her know that he was fine. Spontaneous combustion wasn't super common among his people, although a good number of them had at least had one isolated episode. But for him, these things happened. Of course, Fire bodies were able to withstand it, but it could be upsetting to other Elementals who weren't privy to Fire facts. There were even a few well-known Fires that used it to their advantage and had become Hollywood stunt men and women.

He took a cautious step toward Elms with his hand outstretched to show her that he was indeed fine, even though he wasn't sure he could say the same for his clothing when the smell of burning fabric twirled in his nose. This wasn't the first time he'd flamed up, but it was the first time a woman had been the stimulus. He watched her face contort from panic to abject determination when he was almost able to touch her skin. It was his intention to show her that while she would feel the heat, the flames wouldn't burn her. But without having the words to explain it, she withdrew and did something he had never seen up close and personal. She shifted into her wind element in broad daylight and whirled herself over his heated flesh. *Was she trying to blow him out?* Dear Goddess, having her rushing over his superheated skin was the most amazing feeling. In fact, it was downright *sensual.* Knowing that every single inch of her being was currently washing over him made the fire burn even hotter. Oh man, if she didn't stop this he was going to explode. Explode in more ways that one.

Just when he thought he couldn't take another moment of her running her proverbial fingers over every square inch of him, she lifted him into the air in a funnel cloud of spinning wind. It took a moment for him to realize her intentions, but a few seconds before she let go, it all made sense. Too bad he didn't have the ability to laugh in his current state.

Once she positioned him over the frigid waters of the reservoir, the sensations of Elms surrounding him disappeared faster than they had begun, and he was falling through the air. When he hit the water, his body went into immediate survival mode and extinguished the outer display of his Fire essence and turned it inward to keep him from freezing in the cold waters. He kicked his feet to propel his head toward the surface. With leisurely kicks, he turned until he found Elms standing on the shore. She looked fierce with the sun beating down on her through the trees. In this remote area, snow still covered parts of the ground under large trees, and it reflected the sun to surround her pale skin like a glowing orb. She. Was. Stunning. How was it that he could be mated to someone other than Elms? All it took was one look in her direction and the fire within burned hotter. A single kiss had made him burst into flames.

It didn't matter that Siobhan thought Tiffy would be his fated mate. It didn't matter that Fate never allowed the union of a Wind and a Fire. It didn't even matter that touching Elms might make him explode. He had to. Had to touch her. Had to feel her on his skin. Had to claim her for his own. Fate and the rest of them be damned. Even if it ended with him being the damned one.

One day with her would be enough to carry him through a lifetime with whoever Fate paired him with. Even if Tiffy was Fate's plan. Having made the decision, he dove back beneath the water and swam a lazy breaststroke toward the shore. And Elms. Nearing the shallows, he noticed she'd redressed. Such a shame to cover such a beautiful body. His boots hit gravel and he stood to his full height. That was when it occurred to him that he was missing something pivotal; his clothes.

9.

Playing with fire burns. - Random Thought # 632

Elms stood in open-mouthed wonder at the male specimen before her. Simon looked something that the likes of Rodin and Michelangelo might have sculpted. He was lightly muscled yet slender with a dusting of chest hair that made a beeline right to his... Oh goodness, he was completely naked except for his boots. She tore her eyes back to his face, heat rushing to her cheeks. With every step he took, droplets of water slid free from his hair, ran down his torso, and disappeared into what she could now attest was a decent package, considering the yammerings of old Seinfeld episodes touting the principle of shrinkage.

It wasn't her first time seeing a man in the flesh, thanks to her nursing classes and apprenticeship, but it was the first time she wanted to run her fingers over every inch of one's body and study his reactions. In fact, when she had attempted to put Simon out, her consciousness became hyperaware that each and every molecule of her very being was sliding over and around each smoldering bit of him. Gulp.

At the memory, a flash of heat rushed through her. What was it about him that sent her into a bit of a tizzy? It wasn't like she had a chance with him for the long-term, but as she watched him… stalk was the best way to describe it, her with the look of a starving man seated before a feast, her brain went into a lust-filled overdrive. She watched the water on his skin sizzle, sending small wisps of steam into the air around them.

The temptation to look was too great to ignore, but by the time she glanced down, he had managed to conceal his manhood with his hands.

"Would you mind if I borrowed that blanket?"

His words didn't match his tone of voice. No, his tone sizzled like the water droplets evaporating on his super-heated skin in the February cold. She bent to pick up the blanket and found him close enough to almost brush against when she stood. A shiver coursed through her body as she handed the blanket over and one hand dropped its coverage.

"Cold or scared?" The words rumbled like thunder over her heated flesh.

"Both." It was barely a whisper.

"I can fix at least one of those for you." He met her eyes, slid the blanket into his other hand, then knelt to spread it on the ground. "Do you trust me?" he asked as he dropped to his knees on the blanket.

She sighed. "I barely know you."

"But what does your instinct tell you?" He met her eyes, reached his hands to hers, and gently pulled her toward him on the blanket.

She joined him with no further resistance. "I think my instinct is on the fritz."

"Oh?" An easy smile slid along his face and he settled himself more comfortably on the blanket wearing nothing but his Doc Martens.

"Look, it's obvious I'm unmated, but when I'm around you, I seem to get drawn in like..."

She trailed off, knowing that if she uttered the words 'a moth to a flame,' she would be done for. But it was true. He had some mystical hold over her that called to her at the most primal level of her being. Maybe it was because he was the first male Fire Elemental she had ever really known. Or maybe because he was the first male to ever look at her with such yearning in his eyes. Good Goddess, having a man look at her like he needed her to continue existing gave her a rush unlike anything she had ever experienced. And this was coming from a girl who could flipping fly. *Crap-on-a-stick.* She was already done for.

While Harmony boasted a very diverse population of Elementals, she had grown up in a town mostly full of Winds. It wasn't until she had developed her gift on her thirteenth birthday that people even began to suspect a klutz like her could be a healer. Then, after high school, she moved to Harmony to apprentice for Sophie George, who was one of the most acclaimed healers on the East Coast. And while she was flinging herself into her Fate-given gift, she enrolled in the nursing school at her father's alma mater.

Go big or huddle in the corner trying not to lose her lunch at the sight of blood. She was pretty sure that's how the saying went. And so far, she wasn't doing all that bad. Until now. Without the guidance of her mentor, she was kind of up crap's creek without a boat. Who needed a paddle when you didn't even have a boat? Even with all Sophie's texts at hand, Elms was clueless how to help Tiffy. Which wouldn't result in the shining reference she had hoped for from her first solo patient. And getting hot and bothered by that same patient's possibly fated mate... oh there was a special place in limbo for people like her.

"Where did you go, Little Wind?" Simon's voice seeped into her soul and roused her from her thoughts.

"I'm here. I was just thinking that if you were a Wind, I'd be considering the possibility of you being my mate. But since that isn't possible... Well, maybe Fate brought you here to help me help Tiffy."

"Wait. What about Tiffy?" His look went from sultry to confused in a nanosecond.

"It's confidential really, but let's just go with I'm trying to find the reason behind an issue she's been dealing with."

"Ah, that's what the books were for." A look of disappointment flashed across his face for the briefest of moments. "You mean that fireworks display last night? That's nothing. She's probably having a hormonal shift or something that is setting her off. My sister had that happen recently. My mother swears it's a sign that means a Fire's about to meet their mate when it happens. It's typically a one and done thing, so rest assured, Tiffy will be fine."

"What if it isn't a one and done thing? Then could it be something serious?"

"That I couldn't tell you with any degree of certainty, but I bet it settles down once she and her mate bond."

She studied him closely. "And since you're one of her prospective mates, doesn't that mean that it could be worse now that you're here?" The idea of Simon being the cure for Tiffy's problem should have been reassuring, but it settled in the pit of her stomach like a brick wrapped in barbed wire. Oh Goddess, she wasn't even going to stop in limbo if she let this go any further. Nope, she'd be sitting right next to the Devil himself in Hell for this.

"Look, I've been in town for a couple of days now, and when we met earlier, she didn't seem too keen on me, so there's as good a chance as any that I'm not her fated mate."

She focused on his confidence when the resolve with which he answered should have given her pause.

"Well, thanks for enlightening me." She shifted on the blanket and a shiver wracked her body from head to toe. "It was nice meeting you, Simon. I think I'll head out from here and if you wouldn't mind, leave my stuff back at the Americana. I'll grab it later."

She had every intention of shifting into her Wind form and drifting away from the flame that called to her, but before she could call forth the energy, he turned his palm upward and a small fire sprang from the palm of his hand.

"Wait." He reached for her with his other hand. When she didn't pull away, he held her hand and guided it toward the flame he held. "I promise you won't get hurt. Trust me?"

The question was evident in his eyes which now glowed almost solid gold.

"Yes." It was a mere breath of a word, an exhalation of all the tension she felt when she looked at him and saw his naked body in all its cold-day glory.

He brought the flame that danced in his hand closer to her waiting hand. Slowly he turned his hand over and slid it over her unprotected skin.

The pain of heat that she expected never came. A heat coursed through her from that point of origin and snaked its way along every fiber of her being, heating her enough that she worried she might explode like Tiffy.

"See. Doesn't hurt."

She moved to withdraw her hand from his grasp, but as her hand slid from his, she was overcome by the coldness around her. Against all the warning bells ringing in her head, she did what her body wanted, and scooted closer until she was firmly nestled against Simon. The contact spurred the heat and flames began to lick at his skin where they touched.

"Does it hurt you?" She had to know.

"Nope. The opposite. Can't you feel it?" He removed one hand so that he could slide it through her hair and guide her head enough to find a perfect slant. He lowered his lips to hers with the gentlest brush of skin on skin and it sent the flames licking at his hand shooting higher and hotter. "You do this to me, Little Wind. Every time I even think about touching you, I flame up. How is it possible?" He shook his head then kissed her again, but this time when she opened her mouth to him, he swooped in with a tentative stroke of his tongue against hers.

"Simon," she moaned, pulling away from his embrace. "You promise you won't burn me?" She looked into his soul and dug around to see if she could catch a single glimpse of his motivation. When nothing triggered her radar, she waited for his answer.

"I promise." Simon rose to his feet and pulled her with him. "Let's get you toasty." A smile tugged at the corner of his mouth and he slid his warm hands to the zipper of her coat. He tugged it down in a rush as the metal grew hot between his fingers. "I can't promise the same for your clothing." He chuckled when the metal tab on the zipper glowed red with heat. He let go and took a step back. "How about I stand here and you undress there? I know it isn't ideal, but neither is burning your clothes off." He watched her face flush a deep enough red to almost match her hair.

"I don't think…" Before she could finish her thought, he was back in front of her with his hands in her hair and his lips against hers.

He knew he was playing dirty, but he couldn't help himself with her. There was something about her that made him want her like he'd never wanted someone before. There was an air of innocence about her that intrigued him. Add to it that tomorrow he was certain Siobhan would force him into another 'date' with Tiffany, and then possibly expect him to complete their bond. Once that ball started in motion, there was no going back for him with Elms. He knew that with as much certainty as he knew he didn't want his sister to be right about Tiffy. He'd never forgive himself if he didn't indulge in his Wind just this once.

Although, a small piece of him felt like a

complete shit for taking this liberty with Elms, knowing he wouldn't be able to make her any promises, but the flames that never caused him pain before were twisting him into a mass of agony every time she pulled away from him. Elms had thrown the idea of them being mates out in the abstract sense of it all, but it was hard to negate the theory when she was in his arms and able to soothe the burning with her touch.

"You decide, El. Take them off yourself, or let me send them flying into the ether in little embers. Either way, don't leave." The desperation in his voice surprised his ears. He had never begged anyone for anything, and yet, here he was, willing to play let's make a deal for her to stay.

"Okay."

She took a small step back and slid the coat from her shoulders and laid it down in the snow beneath a walnut tree. Next, she slid the turquoise cable-knit sweater over her head and let it fall to the ground. Standing in the sun in a pair of jeans and a lacy black bra, she looked like sin incarnate. Using the toe of one boot, she slid her foot from the other, then repeated the movements until her toe socks shouted their neon brilliance from the blanket on which they stood. With one last glance at him, she began to loosen the buckle of her belt and the button on her jeans. He held his breath as she slid the denim from her luscious hips to reveal the tiniest scrap of lace covering her that he'd ever seen in his entire life.

He choked back a moan when she finally

met his eyes full on before letting them drop lower and lower still. Shit. He was naked. How the hell had he lost track of that? But when her eyes returned to his with a snap, it no longer mattered because in that instant he saw his hunger reflected in hers.

"Little Wind, I think it's about time to warm you up."

"Agreed. I'm freezing." She laughed and a shiver rolled through her.

Before she could succumb to the cold coursing through her, he wrapped her in his arms and held her against every square inch of him. Including the inches that were currently throbbing in pain against her stomach. She was so small that he hoped he would be able to keep his promise not to hurt her.

He bent and nibbled at her jaw, savoring the sweet spot of the pulse point below her ear. He traced the artery with his tongue and felt the flames begin to course through her to find their counterpoint in him. His fingers took over where his tongue left off and trailed pathways over bare skin. He made the mistake of looking into those blue eyes that always seemed able to captivate him. Something clicked inside him. There wasn't enough warning to prepare her before he was engulfed in flames from head to toe. He watched fear dart into those endless blue pools. Then it was replaced with something he had never expected to see in her; complete trust. She wrapped herself around him and stood on tiptoe to press her lips against his chin.

"Take me with you." She sighed. "Don't hold back this time. Take me with you." She begged.

The invitation was all it took to send him groping haphazardly for her waist. It didn't escape his notice that her undergarments were drifting off into the air as little flecks of burned material. His hands grabbed at her pale flesh and felt the heat reflected back at him through her skin as he lifted her to his own waist. Her legs snaked around his hips, her arms tethered themselves to his neck, until she was anchored to him. With no debate, he found her lips with his as he sought entrance to her heat. He firmly planted his feet to withstand the shifting balance of their flaming joining. Barely able to contain himself, he pushed into her heat with one swift movement until he was met with a slight pulse of resistance. Oh shit.

"Don't. Stop."

Her voice gave him the last little bit of encouragement he needed to sink into her until there was no telling where she stopped and he began. Holding her tightly to his chest to keep his balance as she writhed against him in a rhythm set by the changing winds around them, he let the fire overtake him. Never in his life had he ever imagined it could be like this, so raw and full of passion. She slid against him, pounding him into the deepest recesses of her being. He grabbed for the last little bit of control in his mind, but she arched her back and let out a yowl. His world shattered into a million embers of light and flame. Then she was gone.

IO.

Guilt can feel like a three-ton load strapped to your back. - Random Thought # 15

～

Elms felt guilty leaving Simon so abruptly, but something wasn't right. She let her mind wander with her as she whirled in her Wind form back to the second story window of her aunt's house. She slid in through the screen and slipped under the bottom panel of the window that never closed tight enough to lock. She rematerialized in front of the full-length mirror in her closet, buck-naked. She inspected every inch that she could see of her body and, sure enough, there were no signs of burn marks anywhere on her skin. Too bad her heart felt like it had been burned to a crisp.

She wasn't sure exactly what happened out there with Simon. What had started as a heated flirtation had escalated into her totally giving away her virginity to a complete stranger. The worst part of it all was that she wasn't sad to see it go. Simon had been amazing. She had felt the impulse within him to stop once he realized that it was her first time, but if he had, she was certain she would've walked away and never looked back—and honestly, the thought of not looking back at Simon made tears well up.

Damn Fate. Why would she craft the scenario to put her and Simon together only to tear them apart? Resignation set in when the answer called from the recesses of her brain. Fate wasn't happy until Elms was miserable.

Now, she was going to have to track Simon down to get her books and clothes back in an epic walk-of-shame-turned-disappearing-act. Unless he left her things by the reservoir, then she could take herself back there and get them without the embarrassment. In fact, then she'd never have to see him again, since he was only going to be in town until he and Tiffy could determine if they were fated. Based on his attitude, she didn't think that was the case, which meant he wouldn't be in Harmony for much longer and her life could go back to normal. Whatever normal was, now that she'd given herself to Simon.

She contemplated the merits of taking a quick flight back to the scene of her wantonness when the ringing of the house phone caught her attention. She grabbed a pair of yoga pants and her favorite Lafayette sweatshirt from her dresser drawers and was pulling the shirt over her head when a knock sounded on her bedroom door.

"Are you home, Elms?" Aunt Sue's voice was muffled by the heavy wood of the door.

Tugging the yoga pants on without any undergarments, she hopped her way to the door and threw it open. "Hey." She stood on tip toe and kissed her aunt on the cheek. "What's up?"

"Elma." Sue's tone held all the disapproval a mother figure's voice could. "Did you come sneaking in through the window again? You know this house has perfectly good doors, right?" Her lips twisted up into a smile as bright as the sun. "Declan's on the phone for you. He said he tried your cell a bunch of times this morning, but he couldn't reach you. He was worried and said something about a stranger on the side of the road..." Sue's smile faded into a thin line as she gave Elms a hard stare.

"Oh, I must have left it in Colin's truck. I'll take it from here," she offered, reaching for the handset.

"Please tell me you didn't pick up a stray on the side of the road, Elma," Sue demanded as she released the receiver in her hand.

"I'd never." Elms shook her head and tried her best to look genuine. It wasn't like she'd picked Simon up on the side of the road, after all. She'd left with him from the diner. That was totally different. She took the receiver. "Thanks, Aunt Sue." She pecked her aunt on the cheek, then spun back into the room with the phone pressed to her ear. "Hey, Declan. What's going on?"

"I was calling to see if you were okay. You had me worried this morning with all those messages about you getting hacked into pieces. What happened?"

"Oh, that was nothing." She laughed despite herself. "I just got a little overzealous about a stranger I keep running into. Turns out he's not the serial killer type at all."

"That's good to hear, because if someone was going to run into a deranged serial killer, I'm sure it'd be you."

Just thinking about Simon sent heat racing through her body like never before. "You're probably right, but he was a gentleman and waited with me until Colin arrived. That's all." She hated lying to her cousin, but the truth wasn't the kind of conversation to be had over the phone. It could wait until whenever Declan arrived back in town. By then, Simon was sure to be long gone.

"Oh. Okay."

Elms couldn't tell what he was thinking, but he sure didn't sound convinced by her account. A male voice rumbled in the background.

"Charlie's with me and he says to get rid of your Jeep, he's tired of worrying that it'll fall apart around you one day."

Laughter edged the words, but Elms could hear the underlying concern in her cousin's voice.

"We'll see. So, will you be home soon?"

"In a couple of days. Charlie and I have some meetings with possible investors. If they come through, we could finally be able to quit our day jobs and run the business full-time."

"Wow. That's great news, Dec." Elms loved that her cousin and his best friend were able to use their gifts in ways to help people, both Elemental and human. It would be difficult for them to create a business that didn't reveal too much of their Elemental sides to the humans, but it looked like they were close to succeeding.

"Hey, how about if we all meet up for line dancing and karaoke on Friday night at The Outpost? Should be fun."

"Ooo, that sounds great. I'll tell Colin to save the date."

Declan chuckled, "For you, I think my friend would save *every* date." Again Charlie's voice rumbled in the background. "Hey, the investors are here, so let me run. I'll call you later, 'kay?"

"Sounds good. Go be productive." Elms smiled as she disconnected the call. The phone rang before she had even begun to venture downstairs. "Hello?"

"El?" Colin's voice was as deep as space and as smooth as melted chocolate, which was fitting, since his gift was being able to shift into the form of a chocolate lab-like mix of a dog.

"Hey, Colin. Did I leave my phone in your truck this morning?"

"You sure did and it looks like Dec's been

trying to get ahold of you."

"Yeah, I just got off the phone with him. Anyway, can I talk you into dropping my phone by later on?"

"Actually, I'm not far. Thought you might need a ride to the garage. I just finished my appointment with the foreman at the quarry about that job." She could hear the discomfort in his voice.

"Thanks, Colin. You know, I think Charlie and Declan are getting closer to opening that PI firm they're always talking about, so a job at the quarry might not be so bad for the short-term. Besides, you can always come here and hang with me to break up the monotony of it." She smiled when she said it, even though she knew he couldn't see her.

"Well, I hope they can get it off the ground soon, El. Being unemployed at the moment isn't doing me any favors. I'll see ya in ten." He disconnected the call.

Thankful for the men in her life, she smiled all the way downstairs with the phone.

"Elma, is there something you want to tell me?" Aunt Sue muted the game show she was watching on TV. "Declan seemed concerned." She let the opening hang heavy in the air, knowing all too well that Elms couldn't leave it just hanging there.

She plopped herself on the couch next to her aunt and sighed. "I did meet someone, and I honestly can't tell you that much about him because it was the strangest meeting ever." She laughed. "He caught me talking to myself the other night and I caught him sneaking through the woods. Between the two of us, we'd make a crazy pair." She paused, wistful. "Then this morning when my Jeep broke down, he happened by and waited with me until Colin came."

"Sounds like Fate is putting him in your path, little lady." Her aunt nudged her shoulder with her own, a wide smile decorating her face.

"Yeah, I would've thought the same thing, especially when I walked into the Americana and her was there too. But it's not Fate, because he's a Fire."

"Don't throw the bubbles out with the bathwater, Elma. It will only leave you wondering where all the fun went."

Sue always had little nuggets of cliché mixed with randomness ready to impart as sage advice even if the science behind it wasn't sound, but Elms smiled at her nonetheless. She was right, maybe there could be something between her and Simon, even if it was only so that Elms could use their secret tête-à-tête as a learning experience. After all, Fate gave her Tiffy as a client, maybe she also gave her Simon as a resource. A very hot, sexy resource. Maybe that explained the pull she felt every time she looked his way. Fate was determined to get her the knowledge she needed to be successful. Or maybe it was that a man finally looked at her like a woman for the first time in her life. Being young and short wasn't a great combination. In her experience, men stayed far away, in case she wasn't of the 'legal' variety, even though she was much wiser than her twenty-one years would suggest.

Before she could delve any further into that thought, the doorbell chimed.

"That's Colin. I think we're going to run a few errands and see if I can get an estimate on the Jeep. I had it towed over to JT's."

"Okay. I won't count on you for dinner. But invite that sweet man, Colin, for dinner if you two decide to swing back this way around six. 'Kay?" She plopped back down on the couch and aimed the remote back at the TV.

"You're the best, Aunt Sue." She leaned down to kiss her aunt's head and then scooted to the door.

Seeing Colin in his human form never stopped surprising her. She had known he was something other than a dog when she first met him, since her gift allowed her to see the true origins of people, Elementals, and some objects even. It had been the most interesting meeting ever, but he had turned out to be a great friend whose easy smile was contagious.

"Hey. Thanks again for coming to the rescue this morning."

"Anytime." He put his arms around her shoulders and pulled her close. "Where are we off to first?"

"If I asked you to take me somewhere without asking any questions, could you do that?" She stepped back so she could watch his face change as the question sank in.

"Sure, why not?" He finally agreed, after studying her as hard as she studied him. "Where to?"

She debated for a moment while clambering up into Colin's pickup truck. "Let's stop at JT's first and see how the Jeep is. Then we can drive up to the reservoir."

"Should I not ask about the reservoir? Or should I be worried that you might have cement boots somewhere with my name on them?" Colin chuckled and backed the truck out of the driveway.

She considered telling him about Simon, but if Declan was making comments about her and Colin getting together, maybe there was a reason for it. The last thing she needed right now was to bring Colin into her confusing man-scapade. Plus, she guessed that Colin, knowing the random way she decided to break into her sexual being, would be nothing short of a huge turn-off. It wasn't like most Elementals didn't sow some oats prior to meeting their intended mate, but she knew first-hand that it didn't make for the best conversation starter if the oats they sowed belonged to someone not in their grounding element. The word 'forbidden' was tossed around a lot in those instances. And why upset a guy who actually might be her mate over a one-time thing? Besides, Simon would be out of her hair and, more importantly, Harmony, soon. She couldn't fathom a good enough reason to upset Colin about a guy that would be nothing more than a memory. An amazing memory, but a memory to be sure.

"You know how scattered I can be. I left some stuff there that I need."

Colin didn't bat an eye and headed into downtown. When they came to the one stop light in all of Harmony, he pulled to a stop and turned to face her directly. "Elms, you'd lose your head if it wasn't attached to your shoulders by your neck. I'm not gonna even ask." He shook his head and his low laugh rumbled through the truck.

After talking to the mechanic who had looked over her Jeep, she was ready to call it quits. Simon had been spot-on when he suggested she might need a new alternator. It was shot and she would be out about five hundred bucks. That didn't bode well for her nonexistent budget. She only made a minimal amount from the healing studio at this point, since technically it was Sophie's business, and she was only an apprentice. Plus, she was steadily accumulating a nice big pile of debt, courtesy of Lafayette College. She grumbled to herself about the prospect of riding a bike everywhere in the snow while Colin navigated the twisty back roads that crisscrossed Harmony. She was going to have to figure something out and quick, so she could make it on time tomorrow for classes.

"I can drive you tomorrow," Colin ventured.

She hadn't realized her grumbling had

spilled out of her mouth into actual spoken words until Colin made the offer.

"But I thought you were looking for a job? Won't that stifle your search if you are driving me all over the place?"

"It would, but I already got an offer to start next week at the quarry, so I've got this week free to drive you all over tarnation until your Jeep is back up and running." He kept his eyes on the road as he spoke. "Would that help?"

"Oh, Colin, it would be a huge help, but I know you don't want to be my chauffeur all week."

"Elms, you helped me find a place to live when I was homeless, and you helped get me enrolled in that online GED class so I could actually have a real life. You know, one with a house, career, a family."

By the last word, his voice had lowered to barely a whisper. Of course with a deep voice like his, it was more of a rumble of thunder originating in his chest than actual speech.

"Colin, it wasn't me that did all that for you, it was you." Without thinking, she reached over the empty center seat and laid her hand on his leg. "You did all that for yourself. All I did was make one introduction." She squeezed his leg for emphasis.

Colin reached down and grabbed her hand, returning the squeeze before he pulled the truck off the side of the road near where Simon had parked earlier that day. He shifted the pickup into park and stared into her eyes. She could see emotion boiling right below the surface, but before she could identify what was the root of the emotion, he leaned closer, then reached across her to open the door.

In that instant, one truth became painfully clear. Colin had been prepared to kiss her, but a scent that lingered on her skin had made him change his mind. Thanks to her crappy-butt gift, she knew that for a fact. So much for keeping her tryst with Simon a secret.

II.

The healing arts are just that... an artful way of trying to heal someone. - Random Thought # 384

∿

"We still on for tonight?" Declan popped his head around the doorjamb to the healing clinic's interior door.

Elms jumped at the intrusion. She had been so focused on the research laid out on the counter before her that she hadn't heard him enter Sophie's house. It was finally Friday, after a long, long, long week. After the episode with Colin earlier in the week, she had done some deep meditation. Well, that, and some artful avoidance.

She was grateful that her classes had taken a good chunk of her time and blissfully kept her under both Colin's and Simon's radars. Tack onto that, one client with a raging case of gallstones (eased with some powdered dandelion root), a handful of ear infections (cured with garlic and mullein oil that she cooked up in a jiffy), migraines (Awake for those), and one super-'plosive Tiffy who refused to try any of the ideas Elms had come up with thus far, including sleeping with Simon. She hated to admit, throwing that idea out there had pained her more than she would ever tell.

When Tiffy mentioned that Simon was still in town and actively courting her, thanks to some amplified feelings they both were experiencing, along with the excessive loneliness when they were apart, it only made sense that they had begun the bonding process, so suggesting they sleep together seemed like a good idea. Unfortunately, the worst part of it all was the depth of Elms' longing for the Fire. She often awoke in the middle of the night, heart pounding out of control, breath seizing in her chest, and tears streaming down her face. Thoughts of Simon eased the attacks at first, but since Tiffy's mid-week confession, thoughts of him only made it worse. So, she began taking melatonin and sleeping with headphones pumping the soothing sounds of Enya into her ears and dreams.

One man down. Another to avoid. Luckily her mother offered to pay for the Jeep's repair bill so she didn't have to rely on Colin for rides all week, which worked out for the best because she wasn't sure she could spend so much time with him and not ask him outright why he had changed his mind the other evening about kissing her. In the few times she had seen him, it was overwhelmingly obvious that something had intrinsically changed between them since her tryst with Simon.

She hadn't heard from Simon himself all week, so either he had confessed his sins and had been banned from speaking with Elms, or he was delving into his budding relationship with Tiffy. Either way, she was fine taking a back seat with the whole situation.

Of course if only her brain could get on board with that and stop allowing the man to drift into her subconscious at every turn. Then maybe she could get an actual night's sleep and really consider how she felt about Colin. After all, Colin was a great guy and working really hard to assimilate into Harmony's community, but there were so many unknowns when it came to him. Maybe she just needed to let go of the romantic notion that Simon would come for her even though they could never be together. Yeah, that was probably the best idea she'd had all week.

Of course that right there was the other problem with Simon. He had left all of her stuff right there in the center of the spot where they had, well, you know. But that wasn't the hard part. Nope. It was the note he had written to her on a napkin and tucked in *Mating Rituals of Fire Elementals*. That was what had been the most troubling. Even now, just thinking about it, a flash of heat washed over her.

"Earth to Elms." Dec was right beside her. "Are you all right?"

"Sorry, I was just deep in thought." Elms ducked her head to avoid making eye contact with her cousin. Even though they hadn't been close before she had moved in with his parents, they had really formed a great friendship and a mutual respect for one another. She had contemplated all week whether or not to tell him about everything going on, and now it felt like decision time.

"Sure."

Dec's smile reminded Elms of the cat from *Alice in Wonderland*.

"Maybe I should call Charlie and have him suss out what's going on with you."

Elms gave him a hard stare. "You wouldn't dare." Besides being a close friend of Dec's, Charlie was a telepath, not that he advertised it or anything, but he'd be the first to admit it was a handy skill to have as a state trooper.

"It doesn't take a mind-reader to know that something's up. You've been acting strange since I got home last night. What gives?"

"If I tell you, you have to promise to keep it to yourself." Elms glanced around the healing studio to make sure no one had appeared and would overhear them. "I met someone…"

"No effing way. Who?"

The incredulous look on her cousin's face was enough to make her regret the last five minutes of her life immediately. She took a deep breath and tried to find the best explanation.

"Just this guy who's in town for a short while. We seemed to have a connection, but it's not gonna work out." She began closing the texts on the counter and returning them to Sophie's massive shelves packed with reference books. Then she moved on to tidying up the front office area before she locked the main door. Anything to keep her moving and busy so Dec couldn't watch her reactions too closely.

"So, this mystery guy rolls into town and you what? Fall for him? There's more that you aren't telling me, right?"

She ducked down the hallway that led to the treatment rooms and Sophie's office to avoid the question altogether. She meandered into the office after cleaning the treatment rooms and closing them for the evening only to find Declan sitting at Sophie's desk with Simon's napkin in his hand. Oh, Goddess, no!

"Care to explain this?" He held the thin paper up by his forefinger and thumb with one hand while pointing to it with his other. When she refused to answer, he continued to read the letter aloud. "'Elms, I waited as long as I could for you to come back, but I get the feeling that I took things too far. Please call me so we can talk. I don't want you thinking what happened between us wasn't special for me. Yours, Simon.' What did you do, El? Please don't let it be what I think it is." He let the napkin flutter from his fingers to Sophie's desk. "Please tell me you didn't sleep with a complete stranger."

The lump that formed in her throat when she saw him holding her letter was blocking her ability to talk, and maybe even her ability to form coherent thoughts. He was across the room and had her chin in his hands, tilted to look her directly in the eyes when he spoke again.

"Please tell me you didn't sleep with him."

She shook her head, trying to dislodge his hold, but he held on. Tight.

"I can't tell you that," she croaked.

"Elma Lynn. What were you thinking?"

She tore away from his grasp and stomped her foot right on his insole before she swung her elbow into his ribs. She might be small, but she was mighty as all get-out. "Who the heck are you to ask? I can do whatever I want with whoever I choose. Last I checked, I'm a grown-butt woman. Besides, there isn't anything between us and there won't ever be. Not that it's any of your business." She snatched the letter and stuffed it into her purse along with a couple of books from Sophie's desk that she hadn't had the chance to look through yet.

She heard Dec's limping footsteps behind her as she made her way through the adjoining door from the healing studio into Sophie's home. She paused and waited for him to cross the threshold so she could lock up behind him. Then flipped the switch for the light over the sink before she left her mentor's house, in case Sophie arrived home before Elms was back on Monday morning. It had been over a week since Sophie had left town and Elms still hadn't heard a peep from her. If she didn't hear something soon, she'd break down and call Sophie's daughter, Gracelynn, just to make sure everything was okay.

Head held high, Elms opened the door to her decrepit Jeep and slid behind the wheel. Declan hopped into the passenger seat and slammed the door without saying a word, which meant either someone had dropped him off or he'd 'flown'. Knowing her cousin, he most likely had smooth talked a woman into giving him a lift. Having the gift of being a pacifier gave him the ability to plant ideas in people's minds as if they had been theirs from the very beginning.

Before she turned the key, Elms offered up a silent plea to the Goddess of motor vehicles—or anyone in the ether that might be listening and have sway over the matter—that her Jeep would start. When the engine roared to life, she sank into the artificial leather seats and smiled. This was the first thing that was going right for her today, but she'd take it. A win was a win after all, as her Aunt Sue said. A smile slipped across her lips and before she could stop it, she was giggling.

"What's so funny?" The perplexed look on Declan's face only made her giggles worse.

"Honestly, I don't know. It's been a weird week, and I'm glad to have a win at this moment." Her giggles erupted into full-fledged laughter until tears slid down her face.

"El, you're one strange bird." Her cousin shook his head and a smile crossed his face. "I can't believe you had sex with a stranger." He laughed and she could sense the genuine shift in his attitude in his aura. "If I'd been a betting man, I would've placed money on you and Colin."

"Oh, don't get me started on Colin." She laughed even harder.

"Wait, what happened with Colin?" Dec's laughter stopped and he stared at her, a look of horror crossing his face. "You didn't sleep with Colin, too?"

Elms choked on her laughter and banged her hands on the steering wheel. The pure horror on her cousin's face was enough to keep her laughing uncontrollably for another solid minute before she could catch her breath and form a semi-rational thought.

"I didn't do anything with Colin, but if what you suggested was true, I'm not so sure it still is." She shook her head and shifted the transmission into reverse.

"What do you mean?"

"He didn't tell you?" She asked as she navigated the vehicle into a turn-around in Sophie's driveway.

"Tell me what?" Genuine confusion wafted off Declan.

"That he almost kissed me on Monday. That is, until he got a good whiff of me post-Fire Guy, and changed his mind."

"Oh, El. What am I gonna do with you?" he asked, shaking his head.

"Keep me forever. Right?" She braked at the end of the driveway.

"Always." Declan met her eyes and smiled. "So, are you gonna dedicate a song to Colin tonight at Karaoke?"

"Oh, Goddess no. I plan on dancing only. There will be no singing coming from here." She gestured at her throat as she steered the Jeep towards Declan's apartment.

They rode in silence until she pulled up to the curb in front of the converted robin's egg blue Victorian home that housed his apartment.

"We'll see." Mischief laced words rolled off his tongue before he leaned over to plant a chaste peck on her cheek. "Colin and I'll be by to pick you up in an hour." He winked at her before closing the door and heading up the front steps.

An hour later Elms stood in front of her full-length mirror debating between a pair of cowgirl boots and strappy heels. The heels gave her almost four inches on her frame, putting her squarely over the five-foot mark, but the cowgirl boots were soft, comfy, and way more practical for line dancing. Truth be told, she wasn't about to let an uncomfortable pair of shoes keep her on the sidelines all night. No sir-ee. After the week she'd had, she deserved to dance off some of her excess energy. She needed it. Better yet, she owed it to herself to cut loose and relax without anyone or anything holding her back.

The crunch of gravel beneath truck tires signaled that her time was up. She stuffed her feet into bobby socks and then into the soft brown leather boots. She took one last glance in the mirror to make sure she didn't have lipstick on her teeth, or worse, her dress tucked into her thigh highs. Not that that happened often, but the last time it had, oh Goddess, it had been at a funeral. Yup, in some circles back in her hometown, she still was known as 'thigh-high Elms,' which was apparently universal enough to comment on her under five-foot stature and the fact that she was a fan of garter belts and thigh highs and not so much of a fan for checking that her skirt wasn't tucked into one or the other before leaving the house. She tossed the negative thoughts from her head with a brisk shake and checked the mirror. If a stamp could be given for a passed inspection in a mirror, she would wear it proudly.

The doorbell rang instead of the expected door slam that went along with Dec's traditional arrival in his childhood home. Huh, must be Colin at the door.

"Elma." Sue's voice echoed up the staircase loud enough to wake the dead.

"Coming." She yelled back as she gathered her favorite fleece-lined jean jacket and the tiny purse that fit just the bare necessities before she skipped from her room. It felt good to be getting out tonight and having something to do other than sit around thinking about Simon and Colin. She bounded down the stairs and crashed into the solid bulk that was Colin leaning against the banister.

"Oops," she giggled while detangling herself from him.

"You 'kay, El?" He reached out to steady her while his grey eyes searched her face for any indicator that she was hurt.

"Oh, I'm perfectly peachy." She giggled again as the nerve endings in her arm bristled at the contact. It wasn't the same lick of heat that Simon's touch left behind, but it wasn't completely unpleasant, either. "Ready to go?" She made the mistake of letting her gaze linger too long when he turned back to the door. Huh, Colin had a cute butt. How had she never noticed that before?

Snow and ice crunched under her boots as she made her way to Colin's cherry red Dodge Ram parked in the drive.

"No Declan?"

"Nah. He asked me to come by and get ya. He said something about running late and us picking him up on the way."

Instead of heading directly to the driver's side, Colin offered his arm over a slick patch of ice and opened the passenger door for her. It wasn't until she placed a foot on the step bar to help hoist herself into the big truck that she considered the potential of flashing anyone within viewing distance her hot pink lacy thong.

The thought no sooner crossed her mind when she heard Colin's breath catch in his throat. Yeah, there was no getting around the fact that he had probably just seen not only the panties, but also the matching garter belt holding her silk stockings in place. There were two ways she could play this off: like nothing happened, or like she felt—embarrassed.

Once she was sure she was fully into the cab, she tucked her skirt beneath her derrière and plopped down in the seat.

"Sorry 'bout that." She cringed and heat rushed to color her cheeks. "I didn't think about the fact that all you boys drive big trucks when I got dressed tonight."

She peeked through her lashes to see a flash of heat stain his olive skin. Oh wow, Colin was blushing.

"No harm done, El." He closed her door and took his time getting into the truck.

"Really, I'm so sorry," she offered again before he slid the key into the ignition.

"El, I'm not complaining. Not by a long shot. I'm just not used to you being so... What I mean is... Ugh, I'm just not used to seeing you like this."

He started the truck and backed down the drive. The familiar rumble of the Hemi under the hood lulled her back to a place where she could pretend she hadn't given her friend a peep show. She should've said she'd meet everyone there and driven her own car. Then if she'd had a wardrobe malfunction, it wouldn't have caused the uncomfortable silence she now endured.

Colin turned down Dec's street and pulled to a stop at the curb a few doors down.

"Let's not mention what happened to Dec, 'kay?"

"Yeah. Last thing I need is him thinking I'm

taking advantage of his little cousin." He stroked his hand across his jaw and turned her way. "I know this probably isn't the best time to mention it, but if you don't mind, I think maybe..."

He was cut off by the sound of Declan knocking on her window.

"Did you forget which one was mine?" He pulled the door open and smiled. "Shove over Elms. I'm not riding in the back, it's too cold for that shit."

She unbuckled and slid across the bench seat until her bare leg brushed Colin's solid jean-clad leg. Was it her imagination, or did he shiver? Whatever he had been about to say was put on hold. The prospect of making it through this night unscathed was getting fainter by the moment. The only thing that could make it any worse was bumping into Simon and Tiffy as a happy couple.

12.

Knocking boots is something entirely different in line dancing. - Random Thought # 89

∿

The thrum of music could be heard almost half a mile down the road. By the time they found a parking spot, Elms was ready to get out of the truck and put some distance between her and Colin. The awkwardness clung to her like cling wrap. He was a friend, and a good one at that, and sure, maybe she had entertained the notion of dating him recently, but here he was, looking like he was barely holding onto his sanity each time his gaze wandered her way. And she wasn't helping things, noticing his butt and the way his eyes reflected the silver of the moon. She needed distance to clear her head.

This was getting more complicated by the minute. What had she been thinking? She couldn't date Colin. She was pretty sure he knew her secret, and she was pretty sure he didn't like it. Top that off with the fact that she was convinced he wanted to ask her about it without outing her to her cousin. And there was no way in this lifetime that she wanted to discuss her sex life with a man who she now might even consider being cute enough to date.

Why? Because look at them. She knew that he knew that she was uncomfortable, but she could also tell that he was committed to at least asking. She could sense his waning and waxing courage with every passing minute.

A beat of silence filled the cab when he shifted the truck into park and turned off the ignition.

Before any of them could fill the silence, Charlie wrenched the passenger door open. "What took you so long?"

"It was El's fault," Dec declared, hopping down from the cab.

"Not true. I was ready to go when Colin got there," she protested.

"Yeah." Colin nodded, laid a hand on her bare knee, and any other words he might've been about to say died on his lips.

"Well, let's get in there. Maureen's saving us a table," Charlie called. He slammed the door and headed toward the bar with Declan hot on his heels.

Alone in the cab with Colin, a chill slithered over her. This couldn't be a good thing. If she was still considering dating Colin anywhere in her body, the chill killed it. She pushed the thought away and tried to find anything to say that would make this less uncomfortable for the both of them.

"Hey, before we go in, I need to ask you something." His hand slipped slowly from her bare skin until it settled between them on the seat. "The other day—is there something you want to tell me? I mean, you don't have to—it's not like I have any claim on you or anything—but I feel like I should ask if you're okay." He paused, breath held, waiting for her answer.

"I appreciate your asking, but I'm fine, and the rest really isn't any of your business."

"I thought you might say that. But, El, if you are starting to consider suitors, I think I should let you know, I'm officially throwing my hat in the ring."

Oh no. This was not going to be the carefree night she had planned. Not at all. Nope, this night was going to go down in the records as the date Fate decided to mess with her even more. Lovely. With the truth staring her in the face, she had no words. Pretending to like him or wondering if he liked her was one thing, but knowing he wanted to date her was another and for some reason the memory of the chill that slid over her skin broke through to the surface once again. It was a blatant contrast to the warmth she craved that Simon had so freely given her.

"I'll keep that in mind." She did her best to force a genuine smile across her face, but it rebelled and she gave up.

"Here, let me help you down outta the cab." Colin shifted away and opened his door.

"It's all right. I can manage on my own." She slid to the edge of the seat as he jumped from the cab. Wasting no time, she threw caution out the window and jumped just like she would if she were wearing slacks. She stuck the landing with as much dignity as she could muster, smoothed her skirt, and hurried off to catch up with Charlie and Dec. And left Colin in her wake.

Being short didn't bother her much, until she found herself in crowds the likes of The Outpost's that evening. There were wall to wall people, and she had no luck whatsoever catching a glimpse of Charlie and Declan. She waded through moving bodies and headed toward the bar. At least from there she might be able to get a seat and better scope out the place.

Pushing through one more group of bodies, she felt the all-too-familiar lick of heat against her backside. She whirled around, heart pounding in her ears. Simon. He was here. Crap on a stick. This night was just going to heck in every way possible.

He wore black slacks, a white button-down, and a black leather bomber jacket. All topped off with his Doc Martens. Goddess, he looked good enough to eat. He caught her gaze and it was as if everything in that moment stopped and stood completely still while white-hot heat flared between them.

"There you are, El. I lost you in the crowd. It's packed tonight." Colin stood before her blocking Simon from view.

She leaned to the left to search him out, only to find him flanked by Tiffy and a dishwater-blond who's features mirrored his in a feminine way. The women closed in on him, severing her line of sight again for a moment. Their eyes met once more for the briefest of instants before Declan added to her blockade.

"Charlie and Maureen have a table for us." He nodded his head toward the far side of the room. When she didn't move, Dec gave her a weird look. "Let's order drinks." He nudged Elms and, when she still didn't move on her own, snagged her hand in his and led her to the bar with Colin bringing up the rear.

She caught the briefest wisp of Simon's aura glowing a bright hunter green before he was completely gone from her sight.

"What'llIgitya?" Eddie, the owner and head bartender, asked when they broke through the crowd at the bar.

"A pitcher of India Pales and four glasses to start," Dec yelled over the music. "You want anything?" He glanced at Elms, the question directed her way, since she wasn't much of a drinker.

"Something strong and sweet," she hollered over the noise.

"Yagotit." Eddie nodded then headed down the bar to the tap. Translating his mumbled words was always interesting.

"You're drinking tonight?"

The confusion on Dec's face was understandable. She wasn't a regular at The Outpost, by any means nor was she a fan of alcohol. She had seen way too many people go overboard and the consequences never seemed to match the fun they had. Besides, it wasn't that long since her twenty-first birthday, and even then she had been okay with not celebrating it with a booze-fest. But, tonight was about to be the exception to her no drinking rule. The awkwardness with Colin was enough to make her consider drinking, but seeing Simon there flanked by Tiffy and another woman was what pushed her over the proverbial ledge. There was no way she was going to be able to get through this night stone cold sober.

"There's no time like the present to try something new." She shrugged and turned back to crowd while they waited.

A country band was playing renditions of greatest hits, and off to the far corner of the stage someone was setting up the karaoke machine. Usually, she'd be squeezing through to sign up for at least three of her all-time favorite songs, but tonight she didn't need to feel the heat of a spotlight on her. There was already a fire simmering in her core and she didn't need anything adding to the rush it gave her.

Declan nudged her shoulder and nodded back toward the bar. Eddie had slid a glass with something creamy looking in it. She sniffed the concoction and the familiar scent of chocolate ticked her nose. She smiled and sipped. Whatever it was, it was pure heaven on her taste buds. She took another liberal sip and followed her cousin to a table where Colin was strategically placed between the only two empty chairs. She closed her eyes and took a deep breath. The decision was made for her when Declan took the seat next to Maureen and left her the one between Charlie and Colin.

She sank into the chair and took little sips while Charlie poured out the pitcher into the four glasses. Colin yelled over the music a toast that never hit Elms' ears. She raised her glass anyway and took another long swig of her chocolaty concoction. The fire in the pit of her stomach roared to life as the drink hit home and her blood began to warm. This wasn't so bad after all. She took another sip for good measure, closed her eyes, savored the taste, and swallowed it in a hurry when the band stuck up the beginning chords for her favorite Big & Rich song.

"Who's dancing tonight?" She stood up so fast, her chair wobbled. Colin palmed the chair and held it steady while she felt her body begin to sway to the music without conscious thought from her.

"Us," Maureen proclaimed and grabbed Charlie's hand, dragging him to the floor.

"Why not?" Dec took a swallow of his beer and linked arms with Elms. "Lead the way."

She paused for a moment to see the look of panic on Colin's face. That's right. He never danced when they all went out. This evening was looking up already. Score one for her.

They steered through the crowd already moving on the dance floor until they found space to move with the group doing a line dance. In four beats, Elms was up to count and moving like the song was flowing through her straight into her boot-clad feet. By the time the chorus came around, she was singing along at the top of her lungs and waving her hands in the air like she was lassoing the biggest bull of her life. Heat surrounded her as bodies danced—bumping, twirling, grinding around and into her. She scooted out of the line and kept dancing at the edge of the makeshift dance floor.

Eyes closed, she chanted along with the lyrics; lyrics that took on a whole new meaning when hands slid to her waist and the press of a male body molded to her backside. A male body she'd know anywhere. Heat licked every spot he touched, in a way she had only felt once before. But there was no way on this green Earth that Simon was the reason for the heat. He was here with Tiffy. Right? She opened her eyes and was confronted with the sight of the light, feminine version of Simon dancing up close and personal with Declan. He gave her a wink, then twirled the blond farther into the crowd of dancers. Elms whirled around and dipped into the crystal blue pools of Simon's eyes.

"How?" was all she could get out of her lips.

He just smiled and gripped her hips more tightly. More possessive. More instinctual. More everything. The burning in her ratcheted up a notch. Wow, he looked amazing two-stepping in time with the song, and the swagger of his hips twisted her brain in ways it should never turn, knowing that he was probably fated to be with someone else. But when he joined in on the chorus with her, she couldn't feel anything other than happiness.

The song ended with a flourish and the band slowed into a sweet slow song.

"Wanna dance?" His eyes twinkled in the dim bar light, mischief tugging at his mouth.

"What about Tiffy? Shouldn't you be dancing with her?" She ignored the way his hands snaked around her waist and secured her to his swaying body.

"Tiffy didn't want to dance." His answer was matter-of-fact and cold as the snow on the ground outside.

"Huh." Her body betrayed her and moved in time with his steps around the floor. His hands scorched a slow and deliberate path from her waist to her hips. Her pulse raced and gooseflesh pebbled her skin.

"So, who's your date?"

"Wait. What?" Did he know about Colin? How was that possible? She herself only knew his intentions less than a half hour ago.

"I've seen you with no less than three guys

tonight. Who are you with?"

"Oh, them. None, really. Well..." She considered mentioning Colin, but it wasn't any of Simon's business. That, and she didn't want to ruin the moment with an explanation of her friend-turned-suitor. "It's just a friends' night out."

He held her closer, his breath tickling her ear. "Good."

He steered them to the outer edge of the dance floor near the back corner of the stage. He twirled them once, twice, three times. When her head stopped spinning, she spotted Declan still dancing with the blond. She was amused to find that the woman wore a scowl while in his arms. Maybe her cousin was losing his edge.

"Won't Tiffy and the blond miss you?"

"Siobhan seems pretty entertained at the moment by the guy that came with you, and I don't want to think about Tiffy right now." He released her long enough to open a back door.

She held her breath and hoped an alarm wouldn't sound. When it didn't, she hesitated, until Simon grabbed her hand and pulled her after him into the night.

13.

Wind really is out of this world.
- Random Thought # 75

〜〜

The night wind fought against him as he pulled
Elms from the bar. Damn, Fate held nothing back.
He held tight to the woman who haunted his every
thought, tugging her further into the night.
Holding her small hand in his, he didn't care that
he shouldn't want her because right now there was
nothing he wanted more.

"Where are we going?" She sounded
breathless. He slowed his steps so she didn't have to
jog to keep up with his long stride.

"I'm not sure, but all week I kept hoping I'd

run into you, and now that I did, I'm not ready to let you go."

The pull on his arm was the only indicator he had that she might be changing her mind. The racing of her heart and the warmth sliding between them that burned hottest where his hand clasped hers, told another story leaning in his favor for sure. These weren't signs of a woman being taken against her will, but her refusal to move gave him no option. "What's wrong, Little Wind?"

"I've spent all week researching Fires and trying to make sense of what I feel every time you touch me, but it doesn't make sense. I'm not supposed to feel the heat on you. Your mate should. I mean, Tiffy. She should."

He watched her face crumple with emotions that he could only guess. She kicked the toe of a leather cowgirl boot into a pile of leftover snow and shivered when little bits of snow flew back on her legs. She looked so small and sad standing there that all he wanted to do was grab her, whisk her away, learn every little thing that would make her smile. That gave him an idea.

"Little Wind, how about we do some first-hand research?"

"What do you mean?" Her eyes met his and he swore a flicker of hope surged between them.

"Well, you think Tiffy's my mate. I think you're wrong. Plus, you still need a Fire to get first-hand account answers, and I want to hear about Winds. Like how you did that tornado thing the other day." He tipped her chin up so he could

watch the emotions she wore so publicly on her
sleeve, in case she leaned toward changing her
mind. He knew the instant she made up her mind
to go with him, because any remnants of indecision
melted away from her face and she intertwined her
small hand with his.

"Where to?"

"Your place?" He asked when he realized
that there was a small chance Siobhan would go
looking for him later, and her finding him and Elms
together would send her straight over the edge.
Especially since Shiv had spent her days scheduling
dates for him and Tiffy left and right all week.
Thankfully he had been able to talk her into
coming with him for a bunch of them. It made it
much easier to have her run interference when he
could no longer stand to listen to Tiffy's stories; a
challenge he often faced until Elms. There was
something so captivating about her, that he
couldn't imagine missing a single word she said or a
glance she'd make. How it was possible that he was
destined to end up listening to Tiffy ramble on and
on about Goddess-knows-what when someone like
Elms was just within his grasp, he couldn't fathom.

"No." Her answer snapped him back to the
present. "I live with my aunt and uncle."

"The reservoir?"

"Oh no. Not that again." Her laugh danced
in the night. "I don't think the forest could survive
it."

"Okay, so where to?" His heart pounded
and the fire simmering in his veins hitched up

about ten notches, to a full-on inferno.

"I have an idea." Elms patted the small bag she had slung across her body and smiled when she heard the unmistakable jingle of keys answer her.

"Lead the way, Little Wind."

"Um, I didn't bring my car. I rode with my friends."

"Shit. I left my keys with Siobhan." He looked over her shoulder at the neon bar signs lighting the night from the building they had just escaped. This couldn't be happening.

His first encounter with Elms had been a whirlwind, much like she was and now this night was ending before it started. No. He wasn't about to let her slip through his fingers again. He'd just have to go in there and lie to his sister. He'd leave her and Tiffy with cab money, but the chance of escaping without feeling guilty was minimal at best.

Shit. Shiv's ability to hold a grudge rivaled that of a ticked off nest of hornets. This was going to hurt—that was a given.

Simon squared his shoulders and squeezed the dainty hand in his. "I'll be right back."

"Where are you going? You can't leave them here without a car. This isn't the city, there aren't cabs that run regularly."

He tuned her out and kept walking toward the front door of the bar with its sparse flower barrels and peeling painted bricks. He wasn't going to let anything stop him from getting even just an hour of time with Elms. He couldn't explain it. Not even to his own consciousness' satisfaction, but there was a burning need inside of him to be near her. Elms made him feel more whole than he imagined he could feel when confronted with the idea that his world was falling apart around him, thanks to his sister and an explosive blond who was eager to sink her nails into him and not let go. He'd do anything to escape from that, even if it was only for a night. Besides, if all went well, one night was all he'd need to build his case against why he couldn't possibly be Tiffy's mate.

"I'll go get my car."

Elms' touch, more than her words, made him stray from his course. He glanced down at her hands on the arm of his leather jacket and could feel the heat all the way through to the bone. What he would give to be able to wrap his arms around her and make her his right here, right now.

"I thought you rode here with your friends?" He tried to make sense of her words, but looking into the endless pools of her eyes, made nothing make sense. Nothing other than his desire to claim her as his own.

"You want to learn about Winds? Well, here's your first lesson." She shrugged out of her jean jacket, handed it to him, then wiggled her shoulders.

He watched as her shape began to blur at the edges.

"Wait here; I'll be back in a few." Her voice trailed off as she completely dissipated, clothes and all, into a dense fog and drifted away from him.

He stared after her until he could no longer

track the very essence of her in the night's darkness.

The noise from the bar reached his ears in stark contrast to the emptiness that engulfed him. The bar-laden front door opened and the beat of a popular line dancing song poured out into the parking lot behind a couple that was huddling together laughing. His pulse raced when he felt the familiar jolt of his twin's brain waves near him. He darted between two large pickups and ducked out of sight before she could see him.

This couldn't be happening. If she caught him alone out here, he'd never hear the end of it. At least if she had found him here with Elms, he could fib about finding an answer for Tiffy's condition. Siobhan wouldn't like it, but that would go over better than him shirking his duty by standing alone in the darkness.

He tried to calm the beating in his chest because he knew his sister would be able to sense it if she got close enough. It was an unfortunate side-effect of them being twins. Twins in the community was a rare occurrence, but when it did happen, telepathy between the twins almost always happened. That was until both began the bonding process with their Fate-given mate.

At least that would be an upside to being mated to Tiffy. Siobhan wouldn't always be in his head feeling and experiencing what he did, and he could finally go without knowing every thought and feeling she had. It'd be great to go a month without living through the pitfalls of his sister's PMS. Awkward was the nicest word for it.

The click of the locks on the truck to his left sent his heart into overdrive. The interior dome light blinked on, and he heard his sister giggle. Oh, hell no. He was not gonna sit here and listen to his sister and that guy who Elms had come with get frisky. Not. Gonna. Happen. He peeked under the truck and, when they disappeared into the truck's cab, took off through the tree line to the street beyond.

He didn't slow down until he was about a half mile down the road and his favorite fire-proof boots started to pinch at his toes. If he was going to make it a habit to be running through the woods, he should invest in a nice pair of sneakers. It wasn't like he couldn't afford them, but they never seemed to suit his flammable state. Well that and maybe the years and years of torture care of his lovely sister about him being a dork. He worked hard to make sure his image didn't fit into the stereotypical computer nerd. Even when teaching classes, he leaned towards a James Dean manner of dressing.

He slowed to a lumbering walk. Out here in the sticks there wasn't even streetlights to light his path, so he stayed as close to the edge of the pavement as he could, but he hoped that he wouldn't become a statistic before Elms came back to the bar.

Shit. He told her he'd wait for her there. Damn it. He had no idea which direction she'd be coming from, and he sure as hell didn't have a number for her. He yanked his smartphone from his rear pocket and pulled up the web browser. It was slow to load and he really didn't have much to go on when it opened the blank page of the search engine. He typed Elma + healing + arts + Harmony + NJ into the search bar and hit go.

He let a whoop fly when the search returned an article imbedded in a holistic health website welcoming a woman named Elma McMillan as its new apprentice healer. He dialed the on-call number and waited as it rang in his ear.

"Hello?"

Just hearing her voice on the line made every second of frustration worth it.

"Elms, it's Simon."

"Simon? How'd you get this number?"

He could hear the roar of an engine in the background.

"I looked it up online. Hey, any chance you'd meet me somewhere other than the bar?"

The pause between his question and her answer didn't go unnoticed. He sucked in a breath and waited for her answer, hoping she hadn't gone and done something crazy, like changed her mind.

"I guess. Where are you?"

"I'm not sure exactly." He glanced around for landmarks or anything that would pinpoint his location.

"I think I misheard you. Did you say you don't know where you are?"

"Yeah. My sister and that guy you came with decided to take the party out to his truck and it wasn't something I wanted to witness."

Her laugh startled him. "I'm sorry. I

shouldn't laugh, but all three are known for hitting it big with the ladies. Who was she with?"

"How the heck should I know? They had been dancing earlier, but hell, I got my ass out of there as soon as I saw Shiv." He laughed in spite of himself. Telling Elms made the humor rise to the surface.

How long had it been since he and his sister had had to sneak around and hide their romantic rendezvous from each other? It had to be years at the very least. He chuckled and felt lighter than he had all week. A few words from his Little Wind and he was a new man.

Light pierced the darkness and cut the night as a dark box roared at him around a curve in the road. He jumped back into the brush at the edge of the road and cursed into the receiver.

"Oh my. Please tell me, you aren't on the side of the road?" Elms squeaked in his ear.

"Well, I was until some idiot tried to run me the hell down." He turned to follow the vehicle with his eyes only to see the brake lights blink on. Then the unthinkable happened, the driver shifted into reverse in the darkness and backed down the road toward him again.

"Fuck." He sank further into the brush, tripped over a tree root, and landed hard on his ass on a cold, hard patch of earth. The vehicle stopped right near where he had been standing.

"Simon? Are you oaky?"

Elms' voice wasn't coming through his phone any longer. He glared into the night and could see the dome light of the truck blink on, shining off her red hair as she leaned across to the passenger's side of the cab. He clicked off the call and just laughed. She definitely kept things lively.

"Are you coming or what?" she called.

What could he do? He picked himself up, brushed the debris from his ass and slid in shotgun. This was going to be one for the books.

14.

*I never quite understood the purpose for a clutch—
and not the cute purses either... -Random Thought #
96*

∾∾

Elms took the curves of the back roads a smidge
wide. It wasn't that she didn't know the roads well,
in fact it was just the opposite. In her two and a
half years living here in Harmony, she had grown
quite accustomed to the hills and curves that led to
and from Sophie's home and healing studio, but
instead of her aging Jeep, she was stuck behind the
wheel of her Uncle Ignatius' plumbing truck. The
truck wasn't her first choice, but her car had flat
out refused to budge and she didn't want to drag

her uncle out of bed to look it over. So, she traded his keys for hers, and 'borrowed' his truck, even though it was a beast to handle.

She took the turn onto Brass Castle Road wider and faster than she should've, causing the tires to catch and spin on some loose gravel. She had to give Simon credit. He hadn't made a sound or uttered a word about her driving. If it had been Declan or Colin riding beside her, they would've been all over her about her being a typical girl who couldn't something so big.

She slowed her speed once she passed the dairy farm and the road began a steady uphill climb. Around the next bend, she applied the brakes harder than necessary, and the truck stalled.

"Damn it." She jammed her foot on the clutch and turned the key. The engine sprang to life. She shoved the gear shift into first gear and prayed to whoever might be listening that she wouldn't stall again on this part of the road. It was all hill here. She eased her foot off the clutch as she applied the gas and panicked when the truck rolled back instead of moving forward. "Ugh. I hate driving a stick." She slammed her foot on the brake, forgetting the clutch, and the engine died again. She closed her eyes and counted to three before trying again.

"Need some help?"

"I think so." She hated to admit defeat, but if she couldn't get the truck moving in the right direction soon, she worried they'd get in a wreck. There wasn't a shoulder anywhere on this road, and the idea of turning the truck around and heading back downhill to try again was insane.

Simon slid over the bench seat and pulled the parking brake. "Climb over and I'll give it a try."

She did as he asked, grateful for his choice of words. Before she had snapped her buckle, he had the truck moving steadily up the hill.

"Where to?"

"Keep going until it levels out and you see a bright pink mailbox shaped like an old Victorian house." She waved her hand forward. "I'll tell you when we get close."

He nodded his head in the darkness and cautiously navigated the dark road. The silence in the cab was deafening. She reached down and turned the knob on the radio until she found her favorite country station.

The DJ announced a commercial-free block of tunes heading their way and Rodney Atkins chimed in with the twang of a guitar and the beat of a drum. Without a thought, she joined in, harmonizing with the chorus and danced in her seat. That's when it happened. Simon took a curve a little too sharp and she lost her balance and wound up with her head in his lap. Heat spread like wildfire over her entire body in a flash. He shifted his foot off the accelerator while she froze in place.

"Is that it over there?" he croaked.

She choked back a giggle and lifted her head. Sure enough, Sophie's mailbox was just peeking out in the line of the headlights.

"Mmhmm." She closed her eyes, tried to hold onto the warmth that left her as soon as she broke contact with Simon.

He slowed the truck and turned into the long drive between thick cover of trees. Elms always wondered why Sophie never cut back the trees that blocked her home/business from easy view. Of course, being that Sophie lived on the land right next to the local community leader's apple farm, it wasn't hard for community members to find her.

The truck bumped down the driveway until the house came into view with only the front porch light shining in the darkness. Simon slowed and began to turn the truck into the small parking area that Sophie had recently gotten paved in front of the house by the main door to the healing clinic.

"Don't park here." She waved her hand toward the back of the house. "Follow the driveway around back, and we'll park back there."

Simon was silent as he followed her directions. When he shifted the truck into neutral and pulled the parking brake, she unhooked her seatbelt and reached over for the keys. She threw open her door and jumped into the darkness. It only took a few steps into the darkness before the floodlight blinked on to illuminate this section of the backyard. She followed the slate stepping stones to the back door.

She jingled the key ring, searching for the key to Sophie's house only to realize that she had her uncle's ring. Of course he didn't have the key to Sophie's house that hung from her keys; her keys that now hung on the peg by the back door of her aunt and uncle's house.

She banged her head against the doorframe.

"Everything okay?"

Simon's voice startled her. She hadn't heard him leave the cab of the truck and follow her down the path.

"I just realized I don't have my key." Her brain was going at sixty mph, while she tried to remember where Sophie kept the hide-a-key.

"It's okay." His breath tickled the hairs at the base of her neck. He ran the back of his hand along her arm, then cupped her hand in his and pulled her away from the door frame. "Where are we anyway?"

"This is where I work. You said we'd do research, and here is the best place I could think of."

"It looks like a house, not a healing studio."

"It's both. The healing studio is an addition with the main door around front. But, Sophie gave me a key for the back door. Besides being my mentor, she's kinda like my mom away from home." She slid from his grasp and walked along the pavers looking for anything to spark her memory. She knew Sophie had told her there was a hide-a-key in the event she needed it, but where the heck had she said it was? Gosh, it had to be months since she last thought about the key. It didn't help that Mr. Tall, Dark, and Fiery was standing so darn close to her, frying every last sensible brain cell she owned.

"Then, why don't you just call her or ring the bell so she can let us in?"

"She's not here; that's why we are. After what happened the other day in the woods, I figured it might be smart not to have an audience."

"An audience would be kinky, Little Wind."

From the corner of her eye, she caught the glimmer of something pink and out of place. She moved closer, only to realize it was the heart-shaped piece of rose quartz that Sophie had placed as a token of affection for her mate. Wait. The quartz; that was it. Elms stepped back off the slate stepping stone nearest to the piece of quartz, knelt to the ground, and dug her small fingers under the edge of the cold stone and pulled. Damn. It barely budged.

"Need some help?"

"Please. I think the key is under this paver, but it seems to be pretty stuck to where it is."

She moved aside and watched Simon pull up his sleeves past his elbows and flex the corded muscles that worked beneath his skin as he pulled the stone from the semi-frozen ground. Her fingers slipped beneath the stone, searched the ground, until her fingers brushed against something metallic. She slid it out from beneath the stone and picked it up. A thick piece of tinfoil was wrapped around the key and it shone in the spotlight like a beacon of hope. She unwrapped it and danced back to the door while Simon held the rock in place. She slid the key into the lock and turned the knob.

Smiling, she reached into the darkness of

the house and flipped the switch for the main kitchen light. Once the room was flooded with light, she re-wrapped the key in the foil and tucked it back in its hiding spot. Simon's eyes sparkled as he returned the heavy piece of slate to the ground and stomped it back into place. To her eyes, it didn't even look like it had been disturbed.

Something about the way he looked at her compelled her to touch him. She reached for his hand and gave it a small tug as she turned back towards the house. When his grip tightened around her hand, she felt her steps lighten. She picked up the pace and led him into the house.

She couldn't explain it, but having him touch her made her feel free. It baffled her deep in the recesses of her mind because she only felt free when she shifted into her natural Wind state before now. Since meeting Simon, she had begun to feel trapped, stifled, and lonely. Escaping in her element, as she often did when she felt out-of-sorts, no longer brought her that sense of freedom and rejuvenation. Instead it compounded the feelings of loneliness. Until he touched her. When he was near, she felt more aware than she ever had in her life.

But when he touched her it was like she was finally *alive*. She felt her heart race as heat tore through her body with every step they took together. Maybe that was his gift? In all the research she had done this week, it was the best explanation she could come up with for how she felt. Was it possible that he was able to make people feel what perfect freedom and harmony felt like, just as she could look at things and understand their base beginnings and how they fit into other things?

She pulled him across the threshold to Sophie's home, turned, closed the door, and locked it behind them. The click of the deadbolt echoed in the empty house with finality. She met his eyes and saw the passion there she had seen the other day.

"Let's go into the healing studio. I have my books in there."

The words hung in the air between them, lame, even to her ears, because she knew all she wanted was to find an acceptable reason to be in his arms and feel the release that she believed only he could give her. She looked at the floor, feeling self-conscious for the first time in a long time.

The heat between them intensified when he moved closer to her. Unable to resist, she peeked up at him through her lashes. The look in his eyes could only be called hunger. She swallowed the lump that was sitting at the back of her throat before turning away from him, making her way through the door to the clinic area.

She led the way into the back office and took a seat behind Sophie's desk. She glanced up at Simon as he lowered himself into a seat opposite her. He looked relaxed amongst the chaos in the room.

"So, what do you want to know?" His voice was steady and calm; so unlike how she felt.

"Let's start with why I feel your heat.

Everything I've read said I shouldn't feel it. Especially since I'm not a Fire." She pulled out the steno pad and pen and waited to take notes.

"I'm not sure. I thought maybe you were an empath, because I've never had anyone feel it that wasn't a Fire either. None of my full-human girlfriends have noticed it before. But to be fair, I never flamed out like that with any of them either."

"So, you've dated outside of the community without these issues in the past?"

"Yeah. Not often, but sometimes it was nice not having the expectation of mating after one date. Of course, there is the downside to dating full-humans, too. But I'm usually too busy with work to spend much time dating; seriously or otherwise."

"Well, now you have Tiffy, so I guess that's getting pretty serious." She didn't dare look him in the eyes while she waited for his response.

"That's what Siobhan keeps telling me." His sigh weighed heavy in the small office. "I just have a hard time believing that I'm fated to be with someone so..."

She could feel his brain trying to find the right words.

"Unlike me. We aren't even different enough to be opposites. We're a bad fit, but it's hard to ignore the changes happening with the both of us."

"About that... You and Tiffy are my first Fires, so if it isn't too personal, can you tell me what the bonding process is like for you?"

"I'm sure it's like how it is with Winds. You

feel more intense... aware... alive... But there's the feeling of loss, too—if we're too far away or something. Of course, I'm lucky with that, though. Shiv and I have always had this twin connection, so if she's near Tiffy, I sorta feel the symptoms of the bond, kinda like if I was there myself. It might change once Shiv finds her mate, but for now it's nice for me. I don't have to spend all that much time with Tiffy, and I don't suffer the loss so much."

She digested every word he said and tried to make sense of them. 'Alive' had been an interesting word choice, considering she had used the same word when she tried to explain her reaction to Simon. Everything he was explaining was similar to the accounts she had heard from mated Winds. She scribbled a few notes on the pad in front of her and studied the man before her.

"Have you and your sister always had that type of connection?"

"Yeah. Long as I can remember."

"Maybe having her nearby is interfering with your connection? Like electrical interference or something." Her experience with twin Elementals was about as vast as her experience with pig farming. And she knew nothing about raising no pigs.

He shrugged. The silence shattered with the harsh ringing of the office phone, sending her heart rate soaring. Who knew she was here at this hour? She glanced at the clock mounted over the office door and decided to let it go to voicemail. At this time of the night, no one would be expecting her or Sophie to answer on the office line. If she had to guess, she'd go with someone calling to leave a message, because if it was an emergency, they'd call the after-hours number which was currently being routed to her cell.

Elms listened to the whirl and click of the old-school answering machine that Sophie insisted on using for the office. The recorded message was Sophie's voice. Hearing her mentor's voice was like a soothing balm. She smiled, when after the outgoing message ended, a beep sounded and Sophie's voice came over the line.

"Hi, El. I just wanted to let you know that I'll be back in town next week. I think Gracie will be joining us later in the week. Turns out, her emergency is a late blooming. Although it does create a host of new complications that I hope Isaac can address." A slight pause quieted the room like her mentor had become lost in thought. "Anyway, I wanted to update you on my return. I hope everything is going smoothly for you. I'm certain whatever comes your way, you will handle with no problem. I believe in you. Talk to you soon." Her voice trailed off before the quiet click of her disconnecting the call would be heard on the tape.

Sophie's homecoming would make her life a heck of a lot easier, but Elms could tell that whatever her mentor was dealing with had to be more than 'the usual.'

Her daughter Gracie was what people referred to as a half-breed. While Sophie was a pure-bred and very skilled Wind, Gracie's dad was a mystery. Sophie never spoke of her ex. Ever. And when Gracie didn't come into her gifts on her thirteenth birthday like all the other pure-bred Elemental kids did, it had been the straw that broke the child's back.

Elms had only met the raven-haired beauty once before, but their meeting had left a lasting impression; an impression that haunted her still.

"So, sounds like your boss won't be back tonight."

Simon's voice, seductively smooth, slid her back to the present.

"Sounds that way."

She hadn't expected Sophie back tonight. That was part of the reason she had decided to bring him here. Well, that and curiosity. What she would give to get her hands on him. To examine him fully—for research purposes, of course.

Her heartbeat beat a quick staccato and her cheeks warmed. Wow. Just the thought of having him bared to her was enough to send her into overdrive. That clinched it. She needed to get out more often. Maybe call some of her friends from her nursing studies class and have a girls' night out. Surely she could meet a nice guy who could take her mind off of Simon.

"Since we've got the place all to ourselves, wanna do an experiment?" He leaned toward her and rested his elbows on his knees. The heat pouring off him wrapped around her, drawing her in.

Good gravy. This man would have her exploding into the night if she didn't watch herself. She took a deep breath and let it soak into her very essence. She could tell the minute the air fully took hold inside of her. Her heart slowed, the heat biting at her was smothered with coolness, and her focus became clear.

"Yeah. Let's experiment." She rose from the chair and led the way to an examination room. She held onto her calm as best she could, but feeling him in step behind her caused a struggle within to keep her cool. Maybe this was a bad, bad, baaaadddd idea.

15.

∿

Simon couldn't take his eyes off Elms' ass. It wasn't a problem he usually had, but the dress she was wearing showcased her lithe legs in a way that almost made them look long even though she was rather short. The sway of her hips hypnotized him. He'd follow her anywhere she went, thanks to those hips. And if he wasn't mistaken, he swore earlier he'd seen a flash of hot pink beneath her dress as she'd dissipated.

He followed her into what appeared to be an exam room of sorts, but it was unlike any he had ever seen before. Instead of the customary bed and medical apparatuses, there was an easy chair and an ottoman both in colors of burnt orange with hot blue accent pillows. In place of the typical sterile looking sink and cabinet, there was a privacy shade that looked straight out of a movie set in the sixties; white with large splashes of red, yellow, and orange. It even had a red silky robe tossed over the top at one of the two sets of hinges. The windowsill was full of plants in different stages of bloom, and on the wall hung what appeared to be a spice rack, although the small dark glass bottles had neatly scripted labels unlike any spices he had ever purchased.

Elms settled on a rolling stool at a small cherry roll-top desk and slid it open while he took a closer look at the plants along the sill. A crimson bloom caught his eye. It was one he'd know anywhere. A flame azalea. How fitting that she brought him into a room with a well-known Fire aphrodisiac. Goddess. There was nothing more he wanted then than to hold her in his arms and see if they'd both go up in smoke. He decided it'd be worth it after a moment of thought.

He plucked an open bloom from the plant and twirled it in his fingers. When Elms gave him a questioning look, he tucked the bud behind her ear. It's blazing color mingled with the red of her hair, creating the illusion of her being flame-topped. How had he never realized how much red hair turned him on?

Without another thought, he threaded his

hand into her hair and drew her up to her full height. A heartbeat, nothing more, passed before he lowered his lips to hers.

The heat surged within him. He closed his eyes, deepened the kiss, bent his knees to accommodate her height, and lifted her in his arms. He pressed her back against the wall of the room. The temperature rose around him as her mouth opened to his urgent probing. He couldn't hold it back any longer. He pinned her to the wall for balance as he urged her to wrap her legs around his waist. He needed to be closer to her. To be inside her. To consume her. No. That wouldn't be enough. He needed her to be his; only his.

When he felt her legs lock around him, he eased her away from the wall and trailed his hands along her outer thighs. Shit. His little minx was wearing stockings and a garter belt. He snapped one of the garter straps playfully against her skin then smoothed away any pain she might have felt with his palm.

He continued his path up her thighs until he cupped the flesh of her delicious ass in his hands. And a thong. Good Goddess. She was going to be his undoing. The lace straps beneath his hands were soft and thin. He bet a single tug could rip it away from the heaven they covered. He nipped at her bottom lip with his teeth, and at the same time, tugged the delicate fabric. It ripped away just as he thought it might. Her gasp fueled him on. He hugged her tighter to him with one arm before he dropped the torn garment and let his other hand explore her most intimate pleasures.

A soft moan escaped her lips and hit him right in the heart. This… This right here. It was everything. Everything he expected meeting his mate would be like. Everything he expected falling in love would be like. Everything he expected his world could be like. And it was hand-delivered to him on a sigh by a red-headed Wind that he wasn't allowed to have. Nothing about this was fair even though he had stopped believing in fairness a long, long time ago.

When the hot little number in his arms slid a hand down to work the fly on his pants, he stumbled. He pulled his lips from hers and immediately missed the taste of her. A quick glance around the room left him with little to work with, so he opted for the rolling stool. Two quick steps and he perched Elms on the edge of the stool. Her hands threaded through his hair as his head ducked beneath the hem of her skirt. This was heaven. He inhaled the musky scent of her, drank it in, and let the taste of her dance on his eager tongue. The strain of his heavy erection against his pants was too much. He had to free it. He had to…to…to have her. There was no doubt about it. Ever since their first tryst in the woods, she had been the subject of every dream, thought, moment.

"Simon, we should stop."

The protest was high-pitched and feeble-sounding. He lifted his head from beneath her skirt so he could meet her eyes, but he found them closed. Her face was a bright pink, thanks to the flush his ministrations had caused. He gave himself a mental pat on the back and took the opportunity to capture her lips again. She shivered when their tongues met. He wasn't willing to let the moment pass him by. Sitting back on his heels, he removed his jacket and pulled his shirt off. She was watching him with undivided attention. Standing, he slid his jeans to the ground and kicked them off with his boots. The thunk of his boots hitting the floor was the only sound in the room. It was like time itself was standing still, waiting to see what would happen next.

He took a step toward his Little Wind, careful to watch the emotions play over her face. The moment he saw acquiescence roll over her eyes, he swooped in and swung her up into his arms, pressing her core over his heat. Goddess, he needed her like he needed the air in his lungs. Hell, she might very well be the air his lungs required.

A few steps backward and he felt the press of the armchair on his legs. Lowering them both into the chair, he positioned her opening over his waiting shaft.

"Still want to stop?" He had to be certain. He couldn't betray her like that.

A shake of her head was all it took. He thrust himself into her waiting core and held her there. The fire that had been slowly overtaking his every cell exploded when her walls clenched around him. This was it. He was surely gonna die. At least he'd die happy. Wow. Happy indeed.

She shifted her weight, drawing up from his

lap until he thought she would leave him, only to slide back, drawing him deeper inside. He gripped her hips with tight fingers. The strain of holding back and letting her set the pace was driving him to the edge of his sanity in huge increments.

At the first tremor of her release, he arched off the chair, hugging her to his chest and laid her on the cold floor, not caring a lick about the contrast of it's coldness and his superheated body. He took control and rocked into her with a feverish pace. His climax came soon after hers in a flash of heat. He closed his eyes and laid against her as the fire overtook him, burning hotter than ever before. A flash of light pulsed beyond his eyelids and he could have sworn his entire body shattered into a million and three little embers of fire, but he didn't give it a second thought. All he cared about was the little nymph beneath him.

And that's when the rain started washing over them. Wait. That couldn't be right. They were inside. What the fuck?

Simon opened his eyes and saw Elms trembling on the floor, wrapping her naked body in his leather jacket. Wait. There was no way he was seeing this. One minute ago, he'd been laying on top of her, having the best orgasm of his life, and now he was watching her through some altered universe of time. He was nowhere and everywhere all at once, but an industrial sprinkler system in the ceiling was raining cold water down in the room, putting a stop to burning embers in the fabric of the easy chair. And where were her clothes? He hadn't ever gotten them off of her. Oh shit. He'd burned them off. Time seemed to race, and with blinding speed, all of his molecules crashed into one another, making him solid again. The sheer force of it tossed him to the ground in a fetal position, hoping that he wouldn't vomit.

Fuck. That was intense. For the first time in his life, he'd exploded. And it was all because of a Little Wind.

16.

I'd imagine that attraction, at its most visceral level, is harder to fight than angry hellhounds.
- Random Thought #129

～ッ

The harsh jangle of an unfamiliar ringtone ripped Elms from the best sleep in way too long. She rubbed the sleep from her eyes and strained to make out where she was. Her naked body ached and the darkness confused her for a moment. The memories of the night before attacked with a vengeance. She carefully uncurled herself from the oversized easy chair in the 'Fire' exam room.

Sophie had been smart when she had installed specific features in each of the four main exam rooms tailoring them to the Elemental clientele that would be treated in them. Thankfully, the industrial sprinklers had done their job and contained the small areas of singe that had appeared when Simon had exploded into...flaming snowflakes maybe? It was hard to really explain what she had witnessed. It was a good thing the sprinklers and the discreetly hidden drains had done the trick, otherwise she shuddered to think about how ill-prepared she was for the door and window to seal and the air to get sucked out of the room completely.

Yeah, she wasn't sure if she was as cut-out for this line of work as Fate thought she was. Sophie's practical side far outweighed her emotional side, which made her a legend in the healing arts. But Elms was more heart than head, and that didn't always add up to the best results for the patient. Her nursing school instructors were constantly complimenting her bedside demeanor, but her lack of planning, organization, and overall forethought was a constant ding during practical exercises.

She reached out a hand, felt the wall, and slid along it until she found the light switch. Squinting in the sudden brightness, her heart sank. The room was empty. Last night's events swirled around her brain, mocking her. It served her right. After all, she had left him after their first time together, so he owed her one. In the corner of the room the ringtone sounded again. Hmm. He couldn't have gotten too far without both his pants and boots. She took a slow turn around the room. All of his stuff was still where he had left it, including the jacket she had been curled up under on the chair. Now that she thought about it, she couldn't remember much of what happened after his explosion.

She remembered him disappearing into the flakes of flame. But so did Tiffy...sort of. Tiffy always came back together into one solid being again after an episode, so she was sure that Simon would too. No matter how much she thought it over, she couldn't remember ever seeing Simon come back together. Which left her wondering how she had missed that. Although, in her defense, she may or may not have passed out when the air had been sucked out of the room.

Yeah, not her finest moment for sure, but she couldn't imagine passing out and then sleeping the whole night long like nothing had happened. Right? She couldn't be that bad at her job. Could she? Anything was possible. Especially when she considered the fainting episode at school when they started practicing phlebotomy. Ugh.

The ringing started again, breaking into her thoughts. Maybe it was Simon. Maybe he was stranded somewhere without his clothes and he needed her to come get him. It wasn't like he'd have her number memorized, so he'd have to call his phone.

Elms shook her head dispersing the craziness that overtook her when she thought of him and rummaged through his pants pockets until she found the offending device.

"Hello?"

"Who is this?" If tone was an indicator, the female on the other end of the line wasn't happy. "Where's Simon?"

"Um…" Before she could even come up with an answer, the caller continued.

"Put him on the phone now."

"I would, but he isn't here." Her voice sounded feeble even to her own ears. Confrontation wasn't her strong suit, and it didn't help that she didn't have anything helpful to tell the shrill woman on the other end of the line.

"What the fuck happened to him? I know he's in trouble. I can't feel him any longer. What did you do?" The accusation hung thick in the air.

Guilt washed over her in a wave. The same wave pulled her under when she hit the disconnect button and dropped his phone into one of his boots. She had to figure out what had happened to Simon before she would be expected to explain it to everyone. Especially to his sister and Tiffy. Crappity-crap-crap. What had she done? And where were her clothes? She picked through his pile of clothing only to find her lacy panties torn at the bottom. That's right. Her clothes had burned. Burned right off her body. She took a quick inventory of said body and was relieved to see that her skin bore no tell-tale burns or markings of his heat.

With no other option—well, if one didn't count running through the office and house bare-butt naked as an option, which she didn't—she shrugged his leather jacket on. It hung past her bare bottom, which was a huge plus. This might be the first time being short worked in her favor. She zipped the jacket and ran through the office until she hit the adjoining door to the kitchen and burst through. That's when she realized something wasn't right.

They had left the kitchen light on last night, but all the blinds and drapes had been closed. Yet, sunlight streamed in through the windows and dust motes danced, whirled, and twinkled in the rays. If that wasn't enough, a tea kettle whistled on the stove and two mugs waited on the counter. She turned the burner to off and moved through the house.

Sophie's house was old and every step she took creaked along the hardwoods. When she neared the front of the house, she could hear the echo of water falling coming from the second floor. Then the unmistakable sound of whistling.

Her shoulders dropped and her heart soared. Every pore of her being exhaled with relief. Simon wasn't gone. He was here. She ran up the stairs and tapped on the door to the main bathroom in the house. The whistling stopped.

"Come in, Little Wind."

She opened the door just enough to see the fog-covered mirror. "Did you leave the kettle on?"

"Was it done?" The water stopped and she could see the dark reflection of him through the fog when he opened the shower curtain.

She swallowed, fighting against the lump that seemed a permanent fixture around him in her throat, just as the idea of his naked body covered in water droplets came into a full-color and 3-D apparition. Goddess, the sight of him was enough to make her knees weak. The sigh that escaped her lips was too much. She tried to draw it back, but he had already noticed it, if the smile on his face and the twinkle in his eye was a clue.

A soft chuckle rumbled in his chest when he wrapped a towel around his waist. She felt the heat of him from across the room like it was interlaced with his gaze. His gaze that focused on the fact that she hadn't fully zipped the jacket covering her body. She could feel the heat hitting her right there in the chest. Right where her heart was expanding at too rapid a pace. Right where the knowledge settled that she would never, ever, ever again be the same. Right where her soul soared. Soared into the sky. Soared into oblivion. But it shouldn't. He wasn't hers. He never could be hers. And that's when her soaring soul plummeted back to earth.

She felt the tears waver at the corner of her eyes before the little traitors dripped down her cheeks. If she could dissolve into nothingness right here on the spot, she would, because she didn't dare mar the beauty of what they had shared with her silly schoolgirl feelings. Feelings that she couldn't control but also couldn't deny.

"Little Wind…"

He reached out to brush the tears from her face, and that's when it occurred to her that she, sure as sun on a Jersey summer's day, could dissolve. And with a deep breath, she did just that. Her consciousness watched from wherever it went when she shifted into her Wind form as her solid body dissipated into a fog that shimmered like polished opals. It held onto the leather jacket for one more instant before it slid to the ground feather-like in its decent.

Then the fog rushed off. She knew she would find the rest of her being inside of Sophie's room. The door was always kept closed, as were all the private rooms in the house. Sophie swore it was for energy conservation, but Elms always wondered if it was to keep nosey patients out of personal spaces.

It made sense that her Elemental self would head to the safety of Sophie's private space. It was the most logical place for her to go. There would be clothes, albeit ones too big for her slight frame. But she couldn't take the chance of facing Simon again bared as she was before she got her head in the right place. Being naked didn't help her poor, emotional, and completely unreasonable head.

She materialized into her human form in front of Sophie's closet. Her choices were limited when it came to finding something that would fit well, so she opted for a drawstring umbrella skirt with huge garish flowers all over it, and a simple black fitted T. She considered borrowing some undergarments, but reconsidered almost immediately. There was a fine line she didn't want to cross when it came to borrowing her boss' clothes.

A creak in the hallway alerted her to Simon standing outside the door. She held still, refusing to let even the sound of her breath give her away. She needed more time. Better yet, she needed to remember that he was on loan. Heck, not even on loan. What she had done was the equivalent of pick-pocketing him right out of Tiffy's purse. Craptastic.

17.

I'm only a betting man when I know I'm gonna win. Otherwise, where's the fun in losing? - Random Thought #23

~~

Simon knew something had shifted the night before. He awoke that morning to the surprising realization that he could no longer feel Siobhan. Not that it was the end of the world to not feel his twin for the first time in his life. There was a peace that settled about him, knowing that his thoughts, feelings, and overall sense of self was all his own.

Last night had been nothing short of magical. Of course, he'd never let any of his friends hear him say that shit. Not about a woman.

Especially about a woman as delectable as Elms. Even though he couldn't have her, he didn't want anyone else seeking her out either. If it got back to any of his friends that adding Wind to a Fire would ensure the most earth-shattering moment of your life, he was certain every unmated male Fire on the planet would be lining up to meet her.

After Elms disappeared from the bathroom, he found himself wandering the upstairs hall trying to pinpoint where she had gone. He stopped in front of one of the many closed doors and listened. He heard nothing with his ears, but the heat in his gut flashed up into his chest. His chest that no longer felt so empty. It couldn't be. He hadn't ever felt completely empty until he realized how full he felt at this moment. Without the easy touch of his sister's conscience, he was empty. Until he felt Elms. Something in him knew what couldn't be true. She was supposed to be his. Not Tiffy. Not what his parents had raised him to believe. Not what all the doctrines of his people had taught him over the years.

She was his heart, his soul, his everything. He wanted to tear down the door separating them and pull her into his arms. Goddess, he'd never let her go. Not in a million years. But the eerie silence from beyond the door held him back. Something had spooked her; sent her running. Again. He'd done everything wrong up until this moment. He'd pushed and rushed her, but now he knew he had a lifetime. A lifetime to woo her. A lifetime to wake up with her in his arms. A lifetime of little moments that would paint a happy mated life. The rush to have her imbedded in his mind before he was forced into marrying Tiffy was gone. The pressure to breathe her in and create a lifetime of memories out of a single breath fled. He could have his lifetime. With her. His Elms. His Little Wind.

He decided to give her a moment and headed back down the stairs to the kitchen. He poured out two cups of tea before wandering back into the clinic to find his clothes. Crossing the threshold of the room where they had slept last night was like crossing through a portal into another time. Everywhere he looked were traces of Elms. From the azalea bud on the floor, to the impression of her tiny body still left in the cushions of the chair, to the pile of his clothes with her torn panties now on top. Hmm, she had looked through his stuff.

A metallic beep yelled from his boot. How the hell did his phone wind up there? He was certain it had been in his pants pocket last night when he'd shed them for a slice of heaven. He looked at the readout and saw the familiar pattern of 1's and 0's that was his sister's name in Binary Code. And there were a lot of them. Shit. He didn't even think to call her last night to tell her he wouldn't be returning to the B&B. He'd been so concerned with getting the cold water to stop pouring down on Elms and making her comfortable that he hadn't even given Siobhan a second thought.

He keyed in his passcode and pulled up all

the voicemails. Shit. Seventeen. That had to be a Siobhan record. The first few were all demanding that he return to the bar immediately to drive them home. Then there was one bemoaning him for leaving them without saying goodbye. And another few after she had returned Tiffy home and gotten to the hotel, yelling at him for not answering their door. The next five were all frantic-sounding pleas begging him to call her back because she had woken up and couldn't feel his presence. The last one was like nails on a chalkboard. She demanded to know who "the bitch was that hung up on me." Shit. There was no getting around telling her if Elms had answered his phone. Shit. Shit. Shit. Siobhan was gonna kick his ass for this. She wouldn't understand.

With every inch of his body screaming at him not to call her back, he clicked the redial button.

"What the fuck did you do to my brother?" she demanded after one ring.

"Pretty sure, I didn't do anything to him," he retorted.

"Simon." His name sounded like a gasp instead of a word. "I thought you were dead." He could hear the tremble in her tone. "Are you okay?"

"Shiv, I'm fine," he reassured her the best he could over the phone. "Why would you think I'm dead?"

"I couldn't feel you anymore." She paused and he waited for her to find the words to explain her concern. "Are you okay Si?" Her voice had dropped to almost a whisper. He reached out with all his senses to feel the familiar essence of his sister, only to have nothing answer in return.

"I'm fine Shiv."

"Then why can't I feel you? Could it be the mating? Maybe that's why Tiffy was feeling so bad last night?"

"Oh, shit. Tiffy." That was the moment when his precariously balanced house of fucking cards came crashing down around him. If Tiffy was supposed to be his mate, he'd just doomed her. All for a night with Elms. Fuck. There was no way he would be able to fix this, and now he might be just as fucked as Tiffy. Elemental doctrine warned against breaking the bond between mates because the repercussions often included death. And not natural a death, but depression induced suicide.

"Si? Are you still there?"

"Yeah, Shiv. I'm here. Is Tiffy okay?" Guilt washed over him from head to toe, warring with him from the inside out. How could he be so selfish? He knew better. There had to be something he could do.

"I was able to calm her down. I promised that we'd stop by during her shift this evening." The silence on the line was an entity all on its own. "Si?"

"Yeah, Shiv. What time?" He wracked his brain trying to remember all the teachings from his turning. Goddess, that was ages ago. At least thirteen years. All Elementals came into their prime on their thirteenth birthday. And with that, the lectures shifted from human-focused Sex-Ed to Elemental mating rituals and rights. Being the dumb-ass that he was, he had just broken the cardinal rule. He forgot about the woman he was here to see and, now he realized, supposed to mate with; essentially casting her out and choosing another over her. Not that it didn't happen, but it didn't happen often, and never in his ancestral lineage. Fuck. This was gonna suck.

"She's working the dinner shift tonight." Siobhan's words pulled him out of his head and back to the matter at hand. Tiffy.

"I'll be there." It was as much a promise to himself as it was to Shiv and Tiffy. He'd ask Elms to point him to the town elder. Then he'd beg, if he had to, until the elder helped right his mistake.

"Where are you now? Do you need me to come get you?"

"Don't worry about it, Shiv. There's something I have to do first, but I'll be there. Promise."

"You'd tell me if something was wrong, right Si?"

Out of habit, he buried his feelings to shield them from Shiv before he answered.

"Everything's gonna be fine."

"Okay, Si. Tonight. Seven o'clock." "Yeah. Seven. Promise." He thumbed the off button and pocketed the phone. He felt deflated. A balloon without air. A dog without a bone. A sky without a sun. Elms was going to hate him. Tiffy might already hate him. And right now, even he hated himself a little bit. This day was going to Hell faster than Jack the Ripper had.

18.

When push comes to shove, hope you're the one doing the shoving. - Random Thought # 419

∽

When Elms emerged from the safety of Sophie's room, she was surprised to find no trace of Simon upstairs. The floorboards gave her away as she migrated to the kitchen. What she found reaffirmed what she had come to realize. Last night was a horrible mistake.

Simon sat at the kitchen table, a mug shaking in his large hands. His stare was cold and unseeing. She had grown accustomed to the heat that radiated off of him in waves, but it was nowhere to be found now.

Without a word, she slipped into a chair at the far end of the table. He rose, set his cup down, and retreated to the counter for the other mug. When he returned to the table, he set the cup within her grasp, but none of the warmth she associated with him touched her. Her heart sank into a pit at the deepest part of her being. She watched his body sink into the chair across from her and visibly deflate. It was like someone had sucked the life right out of him. She rolled the memories of this morning through her brain on fast forward, hoping to catch whatever it was that had him looking so dejected. A worry line appeared on his brow and looked all wrong. Almost shocked to find itself on his near-perfect face.

"About last night," he hedged, a frown overtaking his entire face, "I let it get out of control. I'm sorry."

His words stung. They were cold like him. She should've known he'd be upset. He was supposed to mate with someone else and she had interfered. She never should've left the bar with him last night. That had been her first mistake—unless you counted all the mistakes she had made with him before then. The worst part of it all was how he was accepting full responsibility for the disaster they had created. She had known what she was doing when she led him into the Fire room last night. At the very center of her being she had hoped he would make her burn again just so she could remember what it was to feel alive.

His blue eyes had turned to ice. The sigh

that escaped was the only warmth in the room.

"It wasn't all your fault. I knew you and Tiffy were courting. I should never have come here with you." Her voice failed her. She struggled to hold back the tears that threatened to drip down her cheeks. "I'll take you wherever you want to go." She rose from the seat, leaving her tea untouched. Today was turning out to be more of a coffee morning after all.

After she located her purse in Sophie's office, she went straight to her uncle's truck. The sun glittered through the trees and sparkled off frozen patches of snow hidden in the shade beneath them. Usually, this was one of her favorite times of year, when the promise of warmth warred with the chill of winter. In fact, moments like this were usually the bringers of peace in all the chaos in her life. It was too bad that today it only served as a reminder that she, too, was cold, desolate, and alone.

She climbed into the truck and waited for Simon to do the same. Once the engine roared to life, she made the mistake of meeting his cold eyes. Unable to withstand the emptiness in his gaze, she turned back to the driveway and spoke to the steering wheel.

"Where to?"

From the periphery of her eye, she watched him duck his head, almost shrinking inside himself.

"I'm sorry, but I need a favor."

"Shoot."

"Can you take me to your town elder? I

need an audience with him."

She turned the key without a word and jumped from the cab.

"Where are you going? Elms?"

She heard confusion lacing his voice from inside the truck, but she refused to turn back. There was only one reason an Elemental asked for an audience with a town elder. He was planning to ask for permission to complete the official mating ritual. Leave it to the her to open up to the one guy who would turn around and make her show him the way to the alter so he could marry someone else. She should've known. She was a last fling. A wild oat he'd wanted to sow.

Heck, maybe she was just an experiment. They both knew their joining was expressly forbidden by elders all over the globe. Yeah. A good-time girl wasn't how she'd pictured this ending. She padded her bare feet over the cold ground and growled as fallen pine needles stuck her sensitive arches. In the back of her mind she wondered if she was being ridiculous, but the alternative was going back to the truck and being too close to the man she had hoped could be her future. She shook her head against the thought. It was unfair to let her mind play with her heart still, even knowing he was going to marry Tiffy. But why should she care? She knew he was here to meet Tiffy from the moment she saw him in the dark outside the bar. She knew he wasn't hers, and still her brain had done the unthinkable and let her heart get involved enough to begin to hope.

"Elma! Wait!"

His words scarred her. He never called her by her given name. Her broken heart shattered and the tears whipped down her face in hot rivers. The wind picked up around her as she marched to the tree line that separated Sophie's property from Isaac Strom's. She felt the wind embrace her in its consoling arms as she stepped into the woods. She swiped at her eyes.

Crap. She wasn't about to let Simon know he had the power to affect her, and there was no way on the Goddess' green Earth she would let Isaac see her so upset. He could easily read too much into a single look on her face. Without another thought, she shifted into her Wind form, allowing her consciousness to remain behind to see that Simon was able to follow her opal-esque wake.

He thundered through the trees at a run to catch up. When he got close enough to stroke his hands through her mist, she willed her mist form to disperse and a gust of wind shot out of the epicenter of her being. Her awareness watched Simon drop to the ground with hands up to protect his face as pine needles and rocks pelted him. She calmed herself and flowed over the stream bed that held melting ice and marked the border to Isaac's land.

She heard Simon make his way back to his feet, but refused to look back for him this time. If he wanted to have an audience with Isaac that bad, he could just keep up all on his own. She was pretty sure he could take care of himself, if last night was any indication.

She led the way through the trees and seeped into the apple orchard that was Isaac's homestead. She billowed right up to his back door and hung there until Simon rounded the corner of the house.

"Elms." He stopped short in his tracks as her mist undulated by the back door. He seemed to be grasping for the right words. "I'm sorry." A look of pure sadness washed over his face and continued down his sturdy frame.

Her mind considered for one brief minute shifting back into her human form so she could talk with him, but the moment was fleeting at best. There was no way she could face him and not let her feelings show. So rather than give him the benefit of watching her fall apart, she drew her consciousness into her wind, called forth the ambient air, and pulled it into a corkscrew funnel cloud the size of a mailbox. Not big enough to do any damage, but enough to make that point the she wanted him to screw off. At least she hoped, anyway. He was a Fire after all. Maybe he wouldn't understand the symbolism of her gesture.

She tore off back toward Sophie's house, narrowly missing the stubborn jerk who refused to move out of her way.

"I really am sorry," he yelled into the wind. "I wish I could show you how very sorry I am."

His words met her consciousness even though he said them more to himself than to the world. Well, that was too bad, wasn't it? She'd

never give him the chance to show her anything
ever again if she could help it.

19.

What's good for the gander isn't always good for the goose. - Random Thought # 6

~~

"Ahem... Can I help you?"

Simon jumped. He hadn't heard the door behind him open. Before him stood a man of about fifty with dark and silver streaked hair that stood out in contrast against his olive skin. The man wiped his hands on a dishtowel and eyed Simon with accusation in his silver eyes; eyes that were sharp and observant, yet held the kind of sadness Simon felt in the pit of his stomach.

"I'm sorry to disturb you, Sir." He extended his right hand. "My name is Simon Foster and

I'm..."

"Oh, I know who you are." He ignored Simon's outstretched hand, tossed the dishtowel on a counter behind him, and stepped out into the morning chill. "What can I do for you?"

Simon dropped his hand and kicked the toe of his boot into a bit of ice on the ground by his feet. "Well, I was hoping for an audience with the town elder."

"And now you have it." The man's eyes glowered. "So, which of my flock are you here to inquire after? If I am reading you right, you're a Fire. However, I'm pretty sure a certain red-headed Wind almost took out an entire row of my finest producers when she stormed out of here. Are you to blame for that?" He cocked his head to the side. "Or might I be mistaken?"

"I can explain..."

"I can't wait." Sarcasm laced each syllable of the man's words.

The elder was one hard son of a gun. He stood almost as tall as Simon, but he was broader, almost by double. And yet, Simon would've sworn he was at least four times his own size if he were to close his eyes and view the elder as a memory.

"I do have a bit of a sticky situation I'm dealing with, and I was hoping you could advise me on how to proceed." Rather than letting the man get in another word, Simon rushed ahead. "I have a problem. I think I'm supposed to be the mate of Tiffany Reese, but after meeting Elms, well..." He ground his toe deeper into the ice, wishing that the right words would pass his lips to make this man with years of wisdom and tradition at his back understand just how serious his situation was.

"Our Elma does have something about her, doesn't she?" The older man's voice softened. "Of course, you do know that in the history of our people, never have a Wind and Fire been mated. So, I'm a bit confused as to why you're here talking about Elma." A frown hardened his face and lines creased his brow.

Simon couldn't meet the man's eyes. How was he supposed to answer questions that he didn't even have the answers to? Tradition said Tiffy was his ideal mate, but by Goddess, Elms made him burn hotter than he had ever before. Hell, up until this week, he would've been content never meeting his mate if it meant he could focus on his work. He had made it years without needing a steady committed relationship, and now after meeting his Little Wind, he couldn't imagine going back home to his solitary life. But he couldn't imagine going back to his life with Tiffy either.

Shiv had been excited to learn that she and Tiffy had a lot in common. He was certain his sister loved the idea of gaining a partner in crime when he gained a mate. It was a match made in the Ether for her. And yet, the thought of spending eternity with a woman just like his sister was the last thing he could imagine as pleasant.

"Look, I know how confusing it can be to go through the mating ritual."

Simon looked up at the man whose voice

had dropped. The man reached inside the back door and removed a ball cap from somewhere within arm's reach.

"Sir?"

"Call me Isaac," he corrected and placed the cap on his head. Isaac stared off into an elaborate garden that flanked the rear of his home. "Come on." He closed the door behind him and waved at Simon to follow.

They tromped through the brittle winter grass covered in patches of snow and ice. When they entered the garden, Simon was taken aback with what he saw. Shrubs created lines and alleyways, labyrinth-like in their layout, all snaking around what appeared to be a statue of some sort that he could barely make out above the hedges. He followed at Isaac's heels, winding left then right and back again, until they came to a clearing dead-center in the garden. The statue, being more sculpture than an everyday statue, was unlike any he had ever seen in a person's private garden.

A woman, in startling detail—almost as if she was painted in bronze and posed before dusted with stone, looked over her shoulder while holding a painted glass bowl that acted as a birdbath. At the base of the sculpture, the woman's feet were pointed away from the way she was looking, and there was a small heart-shaped piece of rose quartz frozen in the base of the statue. Any Elemental worth their element could tell you the significance of rose quartz. In fact, it was the stone of choice for mated men to buy for their mates. What struck him as odd was the placement of the stone. It sat firmly at her heels so the gaze of her eyes would fall over it, but the sculpted woman was choosing to walk away from the stone. The scene spoke volumes without a word being spoken.

This is a man who knew pain. The kind of pain that lived deep down in one's core and grew hard and jagged with passing days, weeks, years. He had been denied. Simon was almost sure of it.

"Who is she?" Simon regretted the words the minute they left his lips, but he had to know.

"Sophia. She was supposed to be my mate. But she thought otherwise, and I was too young and stupid to do anything about it." He brushed snow from the delicate features for her etched face. "Sometimes you need to do the thing that hurts the most to find true happiness, young man." His hand caressed the stone once more. "I wish I had."

Isaac sat at the stone woman's feet and gestured to a bench opposite him. "Tell me about your situation." He adjusted the cap on his head to shield the morning sun from his eyes.

"Honestly, I'm at a loss. I was sent here to meet Tiffy, but before we met, I had a run-in with Elms..." The memory of her stamping her little foot in the darkness and yelling at Tiffy brought a smile to his face. A smile that he recalled and replaced with a frown.

"Ah-ha. So Elma has caught your attention then?"

"That's an understatement." He paused, letting the realization wash over him. Attention made how he felt sound simple, trite, and overall insignificant, which his heart would deny, even still, at this very moment. Facing the town's elder, knowing he had to ask for Tiffy's hand, and still, all he was doing was thinking of Elms. "What I mean is I think I messed up."

"And how does one mess up a mating?" The words were short, clipped, and the look on his face was anything but warm. "Have you denied your mate?"

Simon felt the color drain from his face. Had he? Was that what had caused him and Shiv to lose their connection? After all, she had been able to feel the bond with Tiffy, too. Oh, Goddess, what had he done?

"I'm not sure."

"You're not sure?" Isaac stood to his full height and glared down at him, accusation stabbing right through to his heart. "Is that why Elma stormed out of here so abruptly? What did you do?"

Bile rose from his stomach, burned his throat, and choked him. How could he have been so stupid? He'd let Elms come between him and his fated mate. And he'd hurt her in the process. The first person to ever make him feel whole, he hurt, all because he wasn't happy with how Fate had conspired to plan his life.

He swallowed back the acidic taste and stood. "I'll fix it with your favor."

Isaac's stare was as hard and cold as the stone of his sculpted ex-love. "You do that. And my favor is in your hands. Don't screw it up."

20.

If my life doesn't flash before my eyes when I die, do I get a do-over on living?
-Random Thought # 219

~⁓

Elms hadn't looked back more than thirteen times during her trek back to Sophie's house. With each turn of her head, dread settled deeper in her soul. Simon wasn't there to ask Isaac for permission to be with her. It shouldn't have taken the thirteenth time of not seeing him following her through the woods to be so sure of it, but it did.

She shifted back to her human form just before leaving the tree line. For once, all her clothes had withstood her transition. The cold beneath her feet matched the ice forming in her heart. What was she thinking? She shook the thoughts from her head, climbed into her uncle's truck, and peeled out onto the main road.

The familiar jingle of her cell sounded from the depths of her tiny purse as she descended the mountain faster than the posted signs advised. Without a second thought, she tore her eyes from the road to locate the small bag and the singing contraption that had slid to the very bottom corner of it.

She hadn't grown up in these parts, but that was no excuse for her stupidity. She knew driving too fast on twisty roads on the sides of mountains was dumb. Maybe even dumber than falling for a guy she couldn't have.

Too bad those thoughts didn't make it all the way into her consciousness before the tell-tale crunch of the metal frame hitting rocks as old as time sounded in her ears. The only thing that registered in her stunned brain as she drove off the road was the overwhelming pain of glass ripping into her flesh as the truck crumpled around her and forged through the trees that lined the road this far up the mountain. The tires bounced on rocks and tossed the truck like a sock on high in the dryer. Her head connected with the paneling of the dash; the thunk reverberating through her thick skull until the noise of it was deafening to her own ears.

Then the uncontrolled motion of the truck stopped as suddenly as it had begun, against a rock the size of a semi-truck. The yet un-shattered pieces of glass joined all the slivers that had already been freed and rained down on her in sharp droplets, but her brain was already unaware. It had blissfully moved on to a higher plane. Or was it a better place? Maybe the Ether? The last flickers of awareness couldn't be sure, but disappointment registered that the only flashes of her life that had bothered to show up before the lights went out, all featured one flame-covered man. Son-of-a-monkey's-uncle.

A bright light bathed her in warmth, washing away the regret and guilt that had plagued her before her death.

"El? Can you hear me?"

A voice deep enough to shake the very foundation of the Ether rumbled through her. How funny. She had always believed Elementals met the Goddess at the end of their journey, since God was too busy dealing with all the humans of the world. The Goddess sounded an awful lot like a man though…

"El?" It sounded more like the letter of the alphabet than her name, but a touch caressed her with the sound. Touch felt awful. It burned and bruised. Maybe she hadn't gone the way of all the good little Elementals. That would explain the pain that accompanied the growl.

The pinch of a blade near her skin registered before she felt her body being dragged through splinters. She heard a wail split the moment. Never did it occur to her that she was the source of it.

"El, I'm sorry. I know it hurts, darlin', but we have to get you out of the cab."

Recognition bloomed. Colin. How?

"Careful! Is she breathing?"

Was that Declan?

"Barely. She's all twisted. I can't get to the belt at her waist without cutting her."

"Let me help."

"Come around to the passenger side. Be careful. It's steeper over there."

"What the hell happened?"

"I don't know."

Hands tugged at her hair and pulled her up against a wall of solid rock.

"She's really heavy for such a small thing. Elms, you gotta help me sit you up. Can you do that?"

The words all rolled through her, making not a lick of sense. Urgency tugged at her, but the lure of the darkness called again.

"Why didn't she shift before impact?"

"I don't fucking know. Can you get the belt?"

"Yeah. Hold her still. I don't wanna cut her."

A grunt washed over her as pain sliced through her head. She needed to get away from the pain. She thrashed against the wall that held her head to the pounding mallet.

"Shit! I said to hold her still!"

"I'm trying. She's shaking. Holy shit. I think she seizing. Where's the fucking squad?"

The blackness took hold and dragged her under. And still all she saw was a flash of fire. *Simon*. Lovely. Just lovely.

"You're lucky your friends saw you go over." An unfamiliar feminine voice stroked her. Pressure pushed and prodded at her body. A body that felt too heavy and sore to really belong to her. A bump and she was jarred from pain to agony. The alien wailing started again.

"Can't you do something for her pain?" Deep as the deepest ocean, the sound rolled over her, washing the wails away.

"Not until the doctor checks her out. Now, sit back down, sir. I can't have you getting hurt while we drive."

Elms struggled to open her eyes, but they refused to obey her brain's request. How very "sorry, try again later" of her brain. A flash of the Magic 8 ball toy she'd kept with her since childhood acting as her brain struck her as funny. Too bad the laugh that attempted to leave her lungs wasn't as amusing. Nope. The chuckle sent a ripple of pain through every fiber of her being. The wailing was back and her head revolted. So did her stomach. Not cool.

"Fuck! What's happening?"

"Sir! Sit down!" The pull of hands on her

body caused another riot in her stomach. "Brad, how far out are we? She's vomiting and her vitals are dropping."

"We're ten out. They're waiting on us."

A familiar tug of warmth spread from her heart and touched every thought that lanced through her head. The warmth lulled her away from the pain and into a sense of serenity.

"Elms, hold on babe. I'll be right with you. Just hold on." The cool deep tones washed the warmth back to nothingness. Blissful nothingness.

21.

Time is a funny little mistress. She whisks away the best of times and drags her feet during the worst of times. - Random Thought # 342

~~

At seven sharp, Simon opened the door of The Outpost. It already was crowded inside. Saturday night in the sticks must make this the only place to hang out. He sought out the familiar blond hair of Shiv and nodded toward the bartender as he made his way to her table. He dropped into a chair with a sigh. It creaked under his weight when he shifted to get comfortable.

Isaac had been kind enough to task a farm hand with driving him back to the B&B after their meeting this morning. On his arrival, the B&B has been quiet without a person in sight. He had taken advantage of the silence and slept for a few hours before he got ready for the inevitable.

After a fitful nap full of images of Elms, he'd gotten in his car, thankful that Shiv had left his key at the front desk for him, and drove. He'd found a train culvert down by the Delaware River and pulled off the road. Something about the way the wind rustled through the trees soothed him. He walked under the bridge out to a rocky shoreline. The peace that settled within him in the time he spent there made getting back into his car easier than he expected.

He hadn't meant to hurt Elms, but he had to do what any good Elemental man would do. He would reestablish the bond he and Tiffy would need to mate and then he would do everything in his power to forget Elms. He owed it to Tiffy, and Fires in general, to mate with who Fate had chosen for him so that he could help further their race.

Of course the minute he laid eyes on his sister, all the bravado he had worked up dissipated. He sat up straight in the hard chair and readied himself for the onslaught he was sure to get. He would be the man everyone expected him to be, even if it hurt. Hurt Elms. Hurt him. Oh, Goddess, this was gonna hurt.

"Where have you been? I've been worried about you all day. I even had to go stay with Tiffy for a while just to make sure she wasn't feeling like shit."

"Thanks. I'm fine, Shiv, and how are you?"
He knew he shouldn't be an ass to her, but misery
crept in as soon as Tiffy's coffee eyes bored a hole
into him from across the room.

"Si, what's going on with you?"

"Nothing." He stole the beer sitting in front
of his sister and took a gulp. Ugh. Lite. A shiver
coursed over his body. He pushed it back at her and
waved a hand to the nearest waitress.

"What can I gitcha, sugar?"

Her southern drawl rolled over him on a
blanket of syrupy sweetness.

"Something strong."

"Ya gottta give me more than that, sugar,"
the waitress purred, laying a hand on his shoulder.

"How about a bourbon, neat? Your sister
mentioned you like bourbon." Nails on a
chalkboard warred for attention with Tiffy's voice
and the heat of her breath at his ear.

The shudder reared its ugly head again.
Fuckin' A. The Southern waitress winked at him
and sauntered off toward the bar.

"Hey, Tiffy."

"Don't 'Hey, Tiffy' me. I can't believe you
flagged down Georgia. She's not like us, you know.
Although, maybe that's your thing."

She shot him a glare that if had been locked
and loaded with actual bullets might have killed
him. This wasn't going well. Shit. It never did with
her. He shook his head, plastered a smile on his
face, and took her hand.

"I'm sorry. I had to have an audience with

Isaac. I'm sure you know him."

His sister glared at him, unable to determine the validity of his statement now that their connection was gone, while Tiffy scraped out a chair and fell into it beside him, shock painted on her face.

"Why? Why would you do such a thing? I was under the impression that you really didn't like me." Her voice softened for the first time since he'd seen her yelling to the heavens with Elms on his first night in town. Goddess, she was almost bearable like this.

He shifted in his seat to face her head on. "Why wouldn't I? We've felt the beginning effects of the bonding process. And I'm afraid what you went through last night might have been an adverse effect of it." His tone dropped and he lifted her chin so their eyes could meet. Really meet. "Had I known it had started, I would've done things differently. And I will from now on." A brief moment of contemplation was all he needed before he leaned in and laid his lips on hers in a soft brush of a kiss. "Promise," he whispered after their lips parted ways.

"Here, sugar." Georgia slid a tumbler in front of him with her sickly sweet smile pasted on her lips. "Tiffy, Eddie's asking after ya." She cocked her head toward the bar and raised an eyebrow.

Simon watched her leave before turning back to Shiv. The look on his sister's face wasn't one he recognized. Hurt, anger, betrayal, incredulity. Maybe a mix of them all in some crazy proportions.

"What?" It felt odd to ask her how she was feeling. She just stared back at him like he had grown another head on his shoulders or something. The general din of the bar began to rise as more and more patrons found their way into the watering hole for the evening. Laughter echoed off the walls and the steady clinking of glasses and beer bottles complimented the country music snaking from speakers strategically placed throughout the main room.

"Where were you last night?"

"With a friend."

"You don't know anyone here. So I'll ask you again. Where were you last night?" Determination took over her facial features. That was a look he knew all too well.

"I met someone. Someone who was trying to help Tiffy with her little explosion situation and I took an interest in it."

"In what? The explosion situation or the person, who I am now guessing is of the female persuasion." She brought her glass to her lips and took a swallow while still pinning him in his seat with her eyes.

He raised his own glass in salute before downing most of it. He used the burn of it sliding down his throat to not think of Elms. "Yeah. A woman. But nothing for you to worry about, sis."

"What did you do, Si?"

"That's not really any of your business, is it?" He countered.

Before she could push further into a discussion about Elms, a commotion rang out by the bar. Tipping back the rest of his drink, he sauntered to the bar to get a better look. The olive-skinned man who he'd seen the night before with Elms was teetering precariously on a stool that was dwarfed by his size. Shit, Simon's fridge back home was smaller than this guy once he got up close.

The human fridge pounded a fist on the bar, yelled for more beer, and tried to unsuccessfully swipe a tear as it streaked down his face.

"What do I have to do to get some service over here?"

"I'm cuttun yuh off, Colin. Yuh had 'nuff. 'Sides, Elms'd tan muh hide if sumptin happened ta'yuh."

Simon's ears prickled at the mention of his Little Wind's name. He glanced over his shoulder as if she might appear out of thin air to agree with the man tending bar, but she was nowhere to be seen in the crowded room. The girl sitting on the stool directly to Colin's left vacated as soon as he aimed an argument the bartender's way. Simon slipped through the crowd and grabbed the seat.

When Colin finally quieted, the bartender turned his attention to Simon. "Whatcha havin?"

"Two of whatever's on tap... and none of that lite crap, either."

"A man after my own heart," the human fridge named Colin piped in.

"Yeah. Lite beer. Who the hell thought that shit was a good idea?"

"Probably some poor sap's wife. 'Hey, honey, if you made one with less calories, we could both drink beer together'." His deep voice cracked when he up-pitched it to mimic a woman. The effect was inspired and hilarious.

"Simon Foster," Simon said, offering his hand.

"Colin DeGrasse. Have we met before?" He shook Simon's offered hand but didn't release it.

"Sorta. I think you helped a friend of mine who was having Jeep troubles." It felt good thinking of Elms, even though he knew he shouldn't.

"That's right. You're El's stalker." Colin dropped Simon's hand as if burnt.

The bartender sidled up across from them with two full steins. He slid them in front of Simon and shook his head in disbelief when Simon slid one in front of Colin.

"He's yuh problem naw."

"Give me your keys." Simon held out his hand and motioned to Colin with his outstretched fingers. "I'll keep your beers coming, long as you hand over your keys."

He wasn't sure Colin would accept the terms, but he caved. He dropped a beat-up key ring into Simon's waiting hand then took a long sip of his beer.

"Look, it's been a shitty day, man. I won't hassle you about El, and you won't hassle me about my drinking."

"Deal." Simon pocketed the keys and sipped his brew. He glanced up into the mirror that backed the bar, surprised by what he saw. Colin had tears running freely down his cheeks. "Wanna talk about it?"

He swiped at the stream with his meaty hands then shook his head. "I fucked up, man. I shoulda told them I was her husband or something. Then I'd be there with her instead of here with you. No offense, man."

"Where with who? Your wife?"

"Nah. El. She wrecked today and once the humans found out I wasn't her relative, they kicked me out."

The air in Simon's lungs froze. His stomach dropped. His pulse raced. No. No, no, no. This couldn't be happening. His blood began to boil. Images of Elms broken and bruised flashed in his head. She was so small and fragile. And alone?

"Where is she?" It wasn't a question. It was a demand. A call to action. An impulse he couldn't control. Shock registered on Colin's face.

"What do you care? Her family's there, and you aren't one of them either, last I checked."

The growl from deep in his chest would intimidate most people, but Simon was immune to it. His Little Wind needed him.

He whipped his cell from his pocket and cued up the app that had made him wealthy. In less time than it took for a mosquito to bite, he had the information he was looking for.

He slid his unfinished beer Colin's way and a twenty across the bar before turning heel and walking out.

"Where the fuck you going with my keys?"
"To her."

22.

Watching someone sleep is like watching grass grow—only more stressful. - Random Thought # 5

∽

The passage of time was just one more item on a long list of things that Elms was unaware of when the door to her hospital room burst open.

"Sir. You can't go in there."

The short, round nurse with the crinkles around her eyes looked familiar, but in the craziness of however long she had been here, she couldn't be sure she actually remembered meeting her. Now the man getting closer by the second, he was another story. His blue eyes blazed as he grabbed her hand and turned his back on the protesting nurse.

"Who's gonna stop me?"

The words, more growl than actual speech, set her teeth on edge. Who was this man and why was he holding her hand so tight? She pulled her hand from his firm grip and took a hard look at his face. He was attractive, she'd give him that, but nothing about him looked familiar.

"Sir, I'm going to have to call security if you don't leave this instant. Only family is allowed on this unit." The nurse stood on tiptoe and attempted to wedge herself between him and the side of the bed.

"Then I'm family," he growled, side-stepping her and reaching to stroke Elms' hair.

"No you aren't." She dodged his caress and was stunned to hear her voice sound fragile, almost in the same way her head felt, just her voice was less banged and bruised.

She had been in and out of consciousness after an accident, the doctor had explained, but the most recent time she had called the nurses' station, the nurse that had come to the room had repeated the doctor's sentiment. Pity dripped off her every word, which didn't bode well for Elms. Three years in nursing school along with her apprenticeship had taught her that when the people taking care of you look at you with pity, things are worse than you think. It was too bad that the pounding in her head hurt enough to discourage thoughts about the state of her current predicament.

"Of course I'm family."

The man's pointed look pierced her chest and a chill took residence in her bones. She rubbed her arms to combat the sensation, but it didn't lessen the weight of his cold stare. A stare that suggested she should understand something that was layered beneath his words, a secret code or something, but her head throbbed and her brain was blissfully blank.

The look on her face must've said enough to the nurse because she unclipped a phone from the pocket of her Eeyore scrub top and placed a call.

"Call security and have them come to ICU room thirteen. We have a man refusing to leave." The nurse slid her lifeline back into her pocket and glared at the man. "This is your last chance to leave without an escort."

"Elms, tell her we are family. Please."

The pleading sound in his voice caught Elms off-guard. She stared at him and tried to understand what he was telling her. Why would a complete stranger want her to lie so he could stay? Her heartstrings tugged underneath the layers of confusion that she wore like a second skin.

"It's okay. Let him stay for a couple of minutes."

"You have until security gets here." The nurse shook her head and stepped outside the door, careful to keep it open behind her.

"I know you're upset with me, but please don't shut me out. When Colin told me you'd been in an accident, I came right here. What happened?"

Regardless how she struggled to recall the

accident, she couldn't pull it from her brain. Her aunt and Declan had been there the one time she woke and told her that she'd driven off the road up near Sophie's house in the early morning hours. But why she would be up near Sophie's so early on a Saturday was a puzzle itself. Sophie always covered the weekends at the healing clinic so Elms could catch up on her homework. The harder she struggled to remember, the more vague the last day registered in her brain—including what might've been a date with her friend Colin that Declan mentioned.

"Look, I'm not sure why you're here, but you only have about a minute until security carts your butt out of here." The stranger's eyes blazed and the corners of his mouth tightened until his lips were devoid of color.

"Elms, please. Just talk to me." He scrubbed at his goatee and looked at the floor. "I'm sorry, Little Wind, I have to give it a go with Tiffy."

"What about Tiffy?" She was thoroughly confused. "What does the waitress at the Post have to do with anything?" The look on his face matched the anarchy in her head.

"Elms, what's my name?"

The look on his face was expectant, but his aura faded to the color of sulfur. Usually she avoided reading stranger's auras because it was an invasion that she refused to inflict. But something about the way he looked at her, helplessness marred with confusion and anxiety gave her the courage she needed to delve into his being. The more she

looked, she noticed the slight tremble of his hands
and an almost imperceptible sway in his stance.
Add to it the fact that his lips had never regained
their color, she knew something was wrong with
the stranger.

"I'm sorry, I don't know your name. I
assume you know me from Sophie's clinic, since
you are obviously having what appears to be a low
blood sugar issue, but as you can see, I'm in no
shape to help you at the moment." She gestured to
the tubes sticking out of her arms and her general
surroundings. Incredulity swamped his aura and his
cheeks flushed.

"Simon." He pointed at his chest. "I'm not
one of your clients. Don't you remember last
night?"

"Last night is a blank."

"What about last week? Sunday night?"

"Gone." She shook her head until the stab
of pain reminded her it was stupid to move the
swelled thing that lived above her shoulders.

She didn't have time to contemplate the
shift of emotions that undulated through his aura
for more than a microsecond, because two burly
men strode through the door and grabbed Simon
by the arms.

He wrenched out of their grip, placed a
heated kiss on her lips, and whispered, "I'll be
back," before the security guards dragged him from
the room.

23.

When the longest Sunday in the history of Sundays goes to Hell. - Random thought # 9,542

༄

The shrill beeping of the alarm clock jolted Simon from his fitful sleep. Before he could curse and find the snooze button in the dark the noise quieted.

"I'm meeting Tiffy for breakfast and then we are headed to Allentown to look at dresses. Don't forget you have a meeting with her parents this afternoon at two."

His sister's voice faded when she shut the door to the on-suite bathroom. The shower cranked up and he heard notes of a familiar song waft from under the door. It was nice to see Shiv so happy for a change, but he could do without her cheerfulness.

He rolled over and shoved the pillow on top of his head to block it all out. His body, limp with fatigue, felt bone weary. The heaviness called him back to dreamland. But sleep had been hard enough to come by after seeing Elms laid up in that hospital bed. The memory tormented him.

The snippets of dreams lingered and churned his gut. Something wasn't right. He shouldn't feel this torn up over someone who had been a stranger a week ago. Especially not when he was supposed to meet his mate's family today to discuss wedding plans; plans that he had been told last night were being made soon. After he had told Tiffy about his audience with Isaac, things had moved forward like Fate herself had her finger on the fast forward button of his life, and his sister wasn't helping matters. Even his mother had called more times in the last twenty-four hours than she had in the last three months.

He gritted his teeth and gave up the idea of going back to sleep. There was too much to do if he was going to stay in town long enough to let the bond take hold. He'd need to arrange for someone to cover his classes at work until he and Tiffy could be married and return to Long Island. They'd have to postpone the honeymoon if he wanted to keep his job, not that he needed it, but he liked the routine of it. Plus, teaching made him be social. Otherwise, he'd stay locked in his home lab and code until he couldn't look at a screen any longer then, shower, shave, and repeat. He'd done it before getting hired on at the University, and it had been profitable, but even then, the few friends he kept in touch with from his days at Virginia Tech constantly harassed him for being a hermit. And not just any hermit, but one that lived at home.

A well-timed intervention was all it had taken to get him to cut his hair, trim his beard, move out, and get a real job. He still thanked whatever star had shined on him the day he interviewed, because he'd worn jeans, a polo, and his favorite worn-in Docs. Somehow, he had still managed to charm the Dean of the technology department enough into giving him the job. Maybe it was the list of programs on his resume that were now well-known enough that people couldn't imagine life without them. Yeah. He didn't need the paycheck, but he loved the faces on his students when he threw his programming credits up on the SMARTboard. You couldn't buy that kind of surprise.

He rolled out of bed, pulled on jeans, and stuffed his bare feet into his unlaced boots. If he wasn't going back to sleep, he might as well get something in his stomach. He scribbled a note for Shiv and slid his phone into his back pocket so later he could hack into the hospital's charting software and get an update on Elms. Just because he was doing his duty as a Fire, didn't mean he wasn't concerned about the Wind.

The Belvidere Bed and Breakfast was bustling with activity for a Sunday morning. As he rounded the corner by the antique carved staircase, the smell of bacon and coffee smacked him upside the head. He inhaled the homey aroma and took the steps at a jog, his laces slapping the steps as he went.

"Good morning, Mr. Foster," called the owner's elderly chef and mother. "Glad to see you up and about so early this morning."

"Thanks, Mrs. Fink. Is the bacon crispy?" He rose an eyebrow in her direction.

"You scoundrel. My bacon is always crispy." Her eyes crinkled around the edges and her false teeth shifted when the smile reached her lips.

The B&B was an old Victorian house that had undergone some massive work to be transformed into the beauty that it currently was. The arm chairs in the parlor were as uncomfortable as they looked and the fireplace was always toasty. But the food... oh, the food couldn't be beat. Not by a gourmet chef. Not by a long shot. Simon selected a dinner plate and piled it high with scrambled egg hash, crispy bacon, and homemade Amish Sweet Bread. He found an empty table by the fireplace amid the hustle and bustle of what was touted as the gathering room. There were more people than could possibly be staying, but no one seemed concerned by the crowd scattered around the room. Simon pulled out the chair, scraping it across the hardwood floor and lowered himself into it with less grace than the old chair was used to, if the protesting creak was an indicator.

He concentrated on eating his food in complete silence, but pieces of conversations drifted around him and tickled his ears. It wasn't until he heard the name Elma that his ears prickled with interest.

"Yeah, I heard she was coming down the mountain too fast. They said she didn't even shift." A woman with salt and pepper hair and a bright purple frock took a long sip from her teacup while her friend digested the words.

"Do you think she was trying to off herself?" The biddy with bottle-orange hair made a slicing motion across her throat to drive her point home.

"Well, you'd think she woulda done *something* had she wanted to save herself."

The words hung in the air, taking a shape all of their own. The gossips passed knowing looks between themselves while Simon choked down his last bite of bacon that had lodged itself in his throat. Maybe there was something to their words. He had seen Elms shift with ease countless times, and if she had, there was no way she would've been injured... Oh shit. She hadn't wanted to walk away from that wreck.

Guilt landed square on his shoulders and gripped him with talons sharp enough to draw blood. What the fuck had he done? He'd somehow allowed her to flutter in and wreck enough havoc that he broke the rules. And not just the ones that didn't matter. No. That would've been too easy. He broke rules as old as time and played with her heart when he knew he couldn't keep her. Maybe their affair had somehow severed a forming bond between her and her fated mate. That would explain why she'd do something so stupid as drive off the side of a mountain for fuck's sake.

He pushed away from the table so fast the chair toppled behind him. He needed to get out of there. Away from all the prying eyes. Away from the guilt that soured his stomach. He took the stairs two at a time and crashed through the door to their suite with precious seconds to spare before his stomach emptied into the wastebasket by the door.

His stomach rolled again, but nothing came up. He collapsed on the floor, head in hand. This couldn't be happening. He had to do something to make it right.

Around noon Simon's phone buzzed with an unknown number.

"Foster."

"Where the fuck are my keys asshole?"

If gravel could growl in English, it would be the noise that was coming through the phone.

"Who is this?"

"How many people's keys have you stolen recently? Where the fuck are they? I need 'em."

The keys in question were sitting on the nightstand beside his own.

"Hey, Colin. Sorry 'bout that man." He ran a hand over an early five o'clock shadow that was beginning to merge with his goatee.

"Don't be sorry. Bring me my fucking keys."

"Yeah. Sure. Where are you?"

He wrote the address on the corner of a magazine and disconnected the call. A quick snap of the camera on his phone and a map and directions were leading the way to the meeting place. Another one of his programs hard at work.

The back roads of Harmony were the only roads of the town it seemed. There was one main artery that ran from Belvidere to Phillipsburg, but it didn't run near the address Colin provided. That's how Simon found himself winding along the back road that paralleled the Delaware River. The morning after he'd first seen Elms, he'd taken this road a la Robert Frost's advice, and it had led him right to her. Today it was leading him to the man that Simon was beginning to believe might be the mate Elms was destined to have.

He neared a curve in the road and veered left, away from the river. A mile down the road sat farmhouses that looked like they belonged in magazines and a solitary log cabin. He turned down the gravel drive of the cabin and cursed his car's low suspension. This kind of terrain hadn't crossed his mind when he'd dropped over a hundred grand on the sports car of his dreams. After bouncing out of a nasty pothole, he stopped the car and decided to walk the rest of the way down the quarter-mile long drive. He left his keys in the ignition and hoofed it with Colin's key ring in his pocket.

As he approached the house, a chocolate lab

growled at him from the front yard. When he didn't stop his course, the dog turned tail and ran in the house through a flap built into the front door. A minute later the Hulk himself stomped out onto the porch.

"What's the matter with your car?" Colin's bellow was loud enough to rival a rumble of thunder.

"Nothing's wrong with my car. Your driveway is the problem," Simon retorted more to himself than the man leaning on the railing of the raised porch.

"Nuttin's wrong with my drive."

The human mountain had the hearing of a dog. Simon shook his head and gave up the fight. "Where's your truck?"

"At the Post, right where I left it. Had to get Eddie to bring me home."

Simon stopped where he stood. "Come on. I'll take you to it. It's the least I could do."

"Damn straight." Colin hurtled the railing and landed with both his feet flat beneath him on the ground. Simon threw the keys in his direction and Colin snatched them out of the air like an eagle grabbing a field mouse.

By the time they reached Simon's Maserati, he was having serious doubts as to whether Colin would even be able to fit his bulk into the passenger seat, but somehow he did. Only there wasn't much room between them to move, let alone breathe.

The quiet of the car was too much for Simon to take, and that's how he'd explain the black eye later.

"Have you heard from Elms?"

"What's it to you?"

Were all that man's words growls? "Oh, she didn't tell you?" Simon cocked his head. He couldn't imagine Elms not at least mentioning him to her friend.

"Tell me what?"

"About us. It was a mistake; I should've known better. Hell, I did know better, but I just couldn't help it. You know what she's like..."

And that was when it happened. Colin's meaty fist made contact with the side of Simon's face and rattled his brain in his skull. He slammed on the brakes and yanked the wheel toward the narrow shoulder of the road. "What. The. Fuck?"

"Don't you dare spread that shit around about El. If I hear another word out of your damned mouth, I will break every fucking tooth in it." A barely concealed rage shimmered over the man vibrating in the seat beside him.

Simon nodded and pulled back onto the road. The remaining five minutes dragged on longer than any in his entire life. Before he could put the car into park beside the red Ram, Colin had the door open and was hopping out of the car.

Simon jammed on the brakes and glared at Colin's back. Colin turned with the speed of a snake about to strike.

"Whatever thoughts you have in your head about El, forget them. Better yet, forget her. Because if I catch you sniffing around, I'll make you regret it." He slammed the door and never looked back.

Shit just got real.

24.

*Family is family and should be protected at all costs. -
Random Thought # 77*

~

Simon didn't know what he expected planning a
wedding to be like, but it sounded like no expense
would be spared to get Tiffy and him down the aisle
before the next weekend was over. His sister flipped
through magazines with his soon-to-be-bride and
mother-in-law. It was all too much and his head
was still throbbing from Colin's sucker punch.
Tiffy's father didn't ask about the swelling on his
cheekbone, just shook his head and handed him a
frozen bag of peas. The women, though, were
another story altogether. They fretted and

demanded he explain.

He made up a story about tripping and his face landing on the desk in their room. Tiffy all but cried that his face mightn't heal in time for the wedding photos. That's how he learned he was going to be married sooner than he thought. While the women cackled around the kitchen table, Tiffy's father gestured to Simon from the comfort of a recliner in the family room. Simon perched on the edge of the sofa and held the defrosting bag to his cheekbone.

"If you don't mind me saying, you don't look like a man ready to commit to his mate." The man looked like his skin had personally weathered all the storms of the past years. He nodded toward a bank of photographs hanging on the wall. "Tiffy's not my first daughter to get mated, you know."

"I didn't know that, sir. Tiffy must've forgotten to mention it." Sheepish as it sounded, he hoped it was true. He had an uncanny knack for tuning out his future wife.

"Son, this is the time here and now to speak up if something's bothering you."

"No, sir. It's been a long day and I'm just not feeling at my best." His phone vibrated in his jeans. "Excuse me for a moment." He slid it free from the confines of his jeans pocket and strode through the front door.

"Dad. Thanks for calling me back."

"Of course, Simon. Your message was concerning."

He lowered himself to the top step and

sighed. "I think I did something horrible, Dad. And not like when I TP'd the principal's house in high school. I mean something that might affect a lot of people for the rest of their lives."

"Slow down and tell me what's going on."

"I think I fucked up my bond," he whispered into the receiver and was met with stony silence. "Dad? Did you hear me?"

"Simon, how could you have done that? What did you do?"

"I met someone. Someone I knew I had no business doing what I did with, but I couldn't help it." He moved from the steps and stood on the curb, his back leaning against his car. "There was something about her that just...I don't know...called to me."

"And I don't suppose she's the woman your mother is all excited for you to be marrying in the next week?"

"No." His head dropped to his chest and he threw the bag of peas he'd still been clutching onto the sidewalk sending little green peas rolling every which way.

"Tell me about it, son. What exactly happened?"

Simon sank to the ground and began at the only place he could; the beginning.

The sound of the front door latching had been what alerted Siobhan to her brother's absence.

Unable to control herself, she parted the curtains beside the front door. She could make out Si's half of the conversation until he left the front stoop and leaned against that ridiculous car that he loved so much. Every inch of her burned to feel their connection again. Without it, she was alone for the first time in her whole life. Well, except for when she and Tiffy were hanging out. Her soon-to-be sister-in-law was a creature comfort she could get used to; as long as Tiffy wasn't drinking. Because when Tiffy drank, strange things happened. Strange things she'd never tell her brother. Like fits of sobbing that ended with sweet kisses. Kisses that awakened a part of Siobhan's soul. Kisses that erased the memory of Declan's hands on her body. Kisses that made her question everything.

A look of shame crossed her brother's face and yanked her from her reverie. Her heart sank. She knew he had been stirring up something over the last week, but he'd refused to discuss it with her. She'd been willing to let it slide since Tiffy and she were getting along so well. The bag of peas exploded on the front walk, and she knew she had no choice but to intervene. Using her Fated gift, she slid quietly out the door and melted like wax to the ground. In her gifted form she was the consistency of oil, the color of liquid gold, and more flammable than jet fuel. It was a common gift among Fires, but she had perfected the level of stealth required to use it for whatever she needed without anyone noticing; human or Elemental.

She slithered over the side of the front

porch and sloshed against a mound of old snow
that looked like it might've been a snowman not
too long ago. She didn't move closer, in case Simon
were to look up and find her hiding spot. Instead,
she held her essence to the confines of an invisible
container and just listened.

"I knew I should've walked away, but every
time I got close to her, all I could think about was
having her in my arms. I know it breaks all the
rules, sleeping with a Wind, but Dad, in those
moments, I was the happiest I've ever been. Until
Shiv told me that Tiffy had an episode that sounded
a lot like strain on a forming bond. That's when I
knew I couldn't keep taking up with Elms. I had to
let her go and do right by Tiffy."

She held herself together and waited while
her father talked from his end of the line out in
New York.

"Yeah, but shortly after I left her to get
permission from the local elder, she drove off the
side of a fucking mountain. She didn't even shift
when it happened, and now she's laid up in a
human hospital with no memories of our time
together."

More silence hummed along her nerve
endings. She wanted to lash out and beat her fists
against her brother. How dare he hurt Tiffy like
that? Better yet, how dare the damn Wind let him?
She knew better, if the Wind was who she thought
she was. Tiffy had mentioned calling a healer
named Elms the night they went line dancing,
when she erupted in pain with Simon's absence.

Of course, now it all made sense. Simon had been with that whore when their connection split, and Tiffy suffered his loss. She couldn't wait to get her hands around his neck. He could've ruined everything with his selfish actions. And for what? A piece of Wind ass? Incredible. She'd never known him to be so careless before.

"Do you think that will help? Okay. I can do it. But are you sure that it won't further damage her ability to bond?" He paused. "I see. Well, that's better than nothing I guess."

Si must've disconnected the call because she heard the car door open and shut before the engine turned over with a purr. Quickly she slid into the wheel well, careful not to coat the brake pads. She was angry with Simon, but she didn't want him dead. That would ruin Tiffy, and then her own chance at happiness could be next. Who in their right mind would mate the woman who killed her own brother for breaking his bond? No one, that's who.

When the car finally stopped, she oozed to the ground and watched her twin from her vantage point under the car. He knelt by something shiny on the ground, lifted a flagstone, and retrieved a key. What the heck was he up to? When he let himself into the back door of the house, she followed, seeping between the old weather stripping on the door and the floor of a kitchen. She oozed into a corner behind a folded step stool.

Simon disappeared through a doorway, his footsteps echoing behind him. He returned with a vial of something a couple of minutes later and stashed it in his pocket. Before she could decide what to do, he was out the door and turning the key in the lock. Well, this was a turn she hadn't foreseen. The crunch of his tires on the drive was her all clear. She shifted into her human form and walked through the door that Simon had entered.

She stepped over the threshold and was surprise to find a huge apothecary. Looks like her big brother was stealing himself a cure for his whore's memory problem. She was certain that's what their dad would've suggested. As the elder in their small reclusive community among the throng of humans, he was always known for doing the right thing. He was a 'high road' kind of guy if ever there was one. She wandered throughout the clinic doing her best to snoop without disturbing things. In the back office, she found a stack of books and a note from the trifling bitch in question.

Hmm, what have we got here? She looked through a stack of papers on the desk. Looks like Si's fling was an apprentice here. She couldn't let this interloper come between her brother and happiness with Tiffy. She wanted what so many others had, and she wanted it now. She flipped through a rolodex until she found what she needed. She pocketed the card with Elms' address and left the office. A bright red door caught her eye near the end of the hall.

She opened it slowly and was confronted with the smell of sandalwood. This was the place. She could smell her brother's soap lingering in the air. Confronted with his betrayal, her heart stuttered. Rage took hold and an idea formed in her head. The innocent looking plant on the windowsill would do. She grabbed three of the open buds and pulled. She slid the address card from her pocket and folded it into a little pouch; a pouch that could hold the crumbled flowers until the perfect moment.

A moment of doubt crept into her mind, but the outrage in the pit of her stomach pushed it aside. There was no turning back now. Her mind was made up. The Wind had to go, and it was up to her to make it happen. After all, flaming azalea was a Fire's best revenge.

25.

When the shit hits the fan—duck. - Random Thought # 56

∾◡

Sunday morning a doctor hustled into Elms' room with a group of interns at his heels. One intern, a tall gangly-looking woman with hair the color of burnt coffee and glasses as thick as bottle bottoms ran through an array of tests. The group concluded her memory-loss seemed to only affect a couple of weeks prior to her accident, but wasn't affecting her ability to store and retain new memories. All in all, it was good news from what Elms could gather. The group shuffled toward her door just as her aunt walked in.

"How's our girl doing?"

The question was directed to the doctors as much as it was to Elms, so she smiled in response and listened to the doctors go through their spiel one more time. The glass walls and pastel-plaid curtains were about to be a thing of the past. She was being downgraded from a trauma ICU room to a standard room on the neurology unit. It spoke of progress that she was fortunate to understand.

"Colin'll be glad to hear you've been moved." Her aunt smiled and patted the arm not hooked up to the IV.

"Why?"

"You probably don't remember, babe." Sue reached down and stroked her hair. "He and Declan found you yesterday morning. He rode here with you in the ambulance and has been worried sick ever since."

A blush crept up her body and left a trail of heat in its wake. Knowing Colin found her set her nerves on edge. Despite the memories that seemed to be missing, she still knew Colin finding her battered and broken had probably been harder on him than it was on her.

He had the misfortune of witnessing his mother's brutal murder at the hands of his deviant grandfather before his fifth birthday. The incident started a trend of him bouncing between foster and group homes until his thirteenth birthday. Like all Elemental kids, that was the day he came into his element and gifts. Only, he didn't have a blood relative around to help him understand the changes; especially the major one that allowed him to take the shape of his current foster family's beloved dog.

Almost two years ago, an underfed stray started following Charlie around while he was investigating a death at Jenny Jump Mountain. When the dog was injured while protecting him from a young black bear attack, Charlie had brought the animal to Sophie. It was Elms that had discovered Colin's secret. She and Sophie had worked tirelessly to bring him back from the edge of death.

Then it had taken Elms months of bringing his animal-self home with her to Sue's and talking to him in his animal form to get him to trust her enough to rejoin society in his human body—and what a body it was. Even though his gifted form had originally taken the shape of a chocolate lab, his human form had grown beneath the canine exterior. And all the exercise his animal form had undergone left him with strong muscles a'plenty. He still preferred to workout in his furred skin, and it boy was it ever a sight to behold.

But years of hiding had taken a toll on him, and you didn't have to look hard to see the battle scars, both on the surface and hidden deep inside his psyche. All those months they had spent together had created a bond that Elms cherished with every fiber of her being. Now, he had a GED, friends who cared about him, and a place that her uncle had helped him build once he had been able to claim an inheritance the state of Pennsylvania had held for him for all those years after his mother died. He had a nice network of friends in the community that had embraced him with open arms, but he oftentimes found his way to Elms' aunt's place.

She struggled to pull the memories of the last few weeks to the forefront of her brain, since Dec had mentioned that she had been with Colin the night before the accident but nothing concrete came to mind. There were only flashes of heat and a deep ache at her core that she had never felt before.

By the time she was moved to her new room on the less restricted floor, she was eager for her aunt to leave. Her body was sore and her head throbbed, but the worst part of it all was her aunt's steadfast refusal to discuss anything of relevance from the last few weeks of Elms' life. Sue swore it was the doctor's orders, but Elms could see the guilt lying beneath every refusal she uttered. Something had happened in the last couple of weeks that had Sue concerned, that much she could divine, but the specifics were locked away in the vault of Elms' mind.

Finally, before dinner, familiar voices wafted down the hall. Declan poked his head around the doorframe and called, "You decent?" before entering her room with a big grin on his face. Colin followed him, a guarded look in his eyes. "We brought you some real food." Dec hefted a paper bag in the air from Toby's.

"Hot dogs." She clapped. "Did you

remember the pickles?" She rolled to her side and grabbed the remote hanging from the rail of the mechanical hospital bed. After pushing a multitude of buttons without success, Colin gently removed the device from her hand and pressed the button to raise the head of the bed, sitting her up. His hands shook when he handed it back then retreated to the farthest corner of the room.

"And the onions and catsup." Dec shivered and tossed the bag on the bedside table and gave her a stern look. "So, you ready to tell us what happened?"

"If I could remember I would." She shrugged and peered into the bag. The first dog she unwrapped had chili and cheese. "Here, this abomination must be yours," she said, wrinkling her nose and handing it to her cousin.

The next one was doctored just to her liking. She tossed the bag to Colin and took a huge bite of the bun-wrapped goodness. She took her time chewing the little bite of heaven and savored the salty flavors on her tongue. When she finally swallowed, she caught the flash in Colin's eyes. His pupils were dilated, darkening his grey eyes to almost black, and she watched his pulse jump in the vein of his neck. He stood against the wall, awkwardly holding the bag, watching her.

This could be the first time she had seen him show restraint around food. He was a big guy, coming in at a solid six foot four inches and built like a professional linebacker. Her mouth went dry when a blush crept up his throat under her scrutiny.

She watched the color of his aura flash a bright fire-orange close to his body. She shook her head to stop seeing the color. Her injury must've knocked out her innate control over her gift. She didn't want to see something so personal on her friend. Especially when he was looking at her.

Her hand shook and she dropped her food onto the wax paper wrapper on her lap. The aching in her nether regions returned with a vengeance. Something on her face must've registered her distress.

"Boys, we should head out and let Elms rest." Her aunt rose and began herding them toward the door.

"Mom, why don't I ride home with you? I think Colin wanted to stick around," Declan hedged. He towered over his mom, but the look she flashed cut him down to her level.

"It's okay." Elms' voice was meek and she refused to meet the six eyes watching her every move.

"All right." An imperceptible head shake was in her aunt's tone as she and Dec left the room.

The quiet descended on her like a thick blanket. She could feel Colin's eyes on her, the weight of his stare suffocating. Courage she didn't know she had bubbled up from the recesses of her soul and she met his eyes. What she saw there matched the flickers of color she kept seeing in his aura and explained his reasons for shifting so frequently. He was uncomfortable, but not because he was nervous like she felt. No, he was trying to conceal the bulge that pressed against the front of his jeans and begged to be released. Under normal circumstances, she would've never noticed it, but his aura drew her eye right to it like a neon sign in the pitch black.

"Can you shut the door? I think we need to discuss a couple of things."

"Yeah, I thought you might say something like that, El." He set the food on the windowsill and turned to shut the door, giving her a clear view of his backside. Had she really never noticed his assets before? He wore his typical uniform of a tee, flannel, jeans, and dusty work boots, but from this vantage point, she noticed that his Wrangler's fit his muscular legs like a second skin. Desire crept from the pit of her stomach, stretched through her veins, and settled low in her abdomen. Where had that come from? It felt so familiar and welcome, but in all her life, she'd never been able to say she actually desired someone, and especially not her best friend.

"What happened, Colin? I need to know and no one seems eager to fill me in." Desperation colored her words even though she fought to keep it buried deep.

She watched the indecision play across his broad face until the answer he needed took root. The bed sank under his weight and the sheets slid lower, revealing more of her hospital gown-clad body. He touched her shoulder, his big hands gentle, and traced one of the many bruises that darkened her pale skin.

"Oh, El, I'm so sorry." Tears shimmered in his eyes while her nickname on his lips tugged at her heart.

"Why?" She didn't remember the wreck, nor did she have any memories that would lead her to believe that he was the reason for her crash.

"I should've come for you sooner. I knew something was wrong when you ran out on me at The Outpost, and instead of trying to find you, I just left you a message and waited."

"Why did I leave? What happened?"

He shifted closer and tucked a wayward chunk of hair behind her ear. "There's something I know I should tell you, but I'm not sure I can." His hand lingered once it hit the bottom of the long lock, the back of his fingers skimming over the rise of her breast.

She stilled and forced the frog that had materialized in her throat back to wherever it had come from. Her pulse betrayed her and raced with the force of a F5 tornado behind it.

He leaned closer, cupped her face with his other meaty hand, and pressed his mouth to hers. His tongue skimmed along the seam of her lips until she welcomed him inside. Any reservations he had disappeared at the first stroke of his tongue on hers. She shivered beneath him.

A coolness swept through her and quelled the fire that had been running rampant through her nerve endings. Her stomach roiled and pain squeezed her heart. She pushed at Colin's chest and sucked in gulp after gulp of air until she could breathe through the stabbing pain that shredded her from the inside out. What was happening?

"El? El? Are you okay?"

The panic in Colin's voice matched the tidal wave of panic that crashed through her and robbed her of the ability to speak, think, move. He was gone before she could take her next breath. His voice echoed in the hall and the sound of running feet registered before hands were on her.

She rode the next wave with tears streaming down her face. The head of the bed dropped under her and hushed voices barked commands. Her muscles contracted into tight knots then spasmed until her body was overcome by the brutal shaking.

A cool rush of liquid swirled through her veins from her IV site with the push of meds. Which ones, she couldn't hazard a guess because the only thing her brain registered was that she had done a bad, bad thing.

Sunday night traffic wasn't bad out in the sticks. Still, Simon took the curves in the road with care. The little bottle nestled in his cup holder was far too precious to end up in a pile of twisted metal. He hoped Elms would forgive him for breaking into her place of work, but since her mentor was still M.I.A., he didn't have another option. His father had come up with a brilliant plan, one that would end with Elms hating his guts, but should repair any tears that might exist in the threads of her bond.

It was funny just how focused he was on bonds at the moment. He'd been perfectly content at home with his house and steady job, until his family pushed him to come to this place. This place that had twisted everything he knew to be true and made fairytales seem real. This place where he now found himself, only then to realize he didn't approve of what he'd discovered. Wasn't that the fucking icing on the donut?

Some people in the community messed around with people of other grounding elements, but it was so frowned upon that not many did it publicly. And still, he'd pursued Elms. He'd chased her without abandon and he took everything she offered with relish. Her innocence, her trust, her bond. He was a rat bastard by all standards for any of those things, but the combination made him even worse than a rat bastard—whatever that was.

He parked in the parking deck at the hospital in nearby Phillipsburg and thumbed through his app. The hospital's digital record-keeping system was easy to hack. A few keystrokes and he had what he needed. He tucked the precious vial into his pocket and entered the hospital. No one took notice of him as he strode through the lobby and took the elevator to the Neurology unit. He checked the digital readout on his phone. It was well within the visiting hours. This would be an easy in and out if all went according to plan.

He turned past the nurses' station and rounded a corner, stopping at room 318. The door was closed, but he could feel her inside the room. Her essence called to him even still. He had to give her the potion before things got worse. He peered through the tiny square window in her door and his heart stopped. His feet rooted to the ground and refused to move. Colin's hand was on her face and he was leaning close enough to fucking kiss her.

Fire ignited in his veins. This wasn't happening. It couldn't be. Colin touched his lips to hers and Simon staggered, his legs buckling beneath him. A blast of ice ran through his veins and his vision clouded. He forced himself away from the door and around the corner. A few more steps and he'd have the privacy of a restroom to lose it. He couldn't do it here out in the open, but the ice growing in his gut was clawing and reaching its dead fingers around each organ it passed, squeezing him until he could barely catch his breath. He used the wall for support and staggered forward.

"Sir, are you okay?"

The voice reached his ears, but it was only seconds before he heard Colin yelling for help. Simon jiggled the men's room door handle, fighting to get it open. When it finally gave, he dropped to the ground and groped for the vial safe in his pocket. Things were going bad and quick.

This was what his father had warned him about. His attraction to Elms might've been against the recorded rules of their people, but it was evident now that it was a twist of Fate's humor. A rip of pain tore at his heart. If he was going to save Elms from this cruel twist of Fate, he had to act now. He wrestled the vial from his pocket. He paid no attention to the word "Forget" scrawled across the faded label, uncorked it, and drank it down.

The bitter taste of the potion coated his tongue then oozed down his throat. He prayed to anyone who'd listen as he waited for the potion to seep into his blood stream and halt the tear that was working its way across his heart. If the tear split his heart, then there would be nothing more he could do. He and Elms would both be subjected to the pain that accompanied a broken bond since that's what was happening. But now, the dangerous witches' potion would be a way to rewind time, as long as he got it to his heart before the bond completely broke. He'd forget her. She already forgot him, and they would go about their lives none the wiser, unless Fate toyed with them again. But he'd be faithful to his promise to Tiffy and, with any luck, he'd avoid Elms doing it.

Fate was a bitch. She had played her hand and he'd ignored her full house. He'd been cocky and gone ahead and bargained with the devil he thought he knew, and he'd ended with two of a kind. Regret tugged at him as the icy blade in his heart began to retreat.

It was working. He could feel it. His heart was still intact, maybe even healing, but with each easier breath he took, he felt her slipping from his memories. Before long, she'd be gone. No memories. No anything. Just an emptiness he'd never be able to fill. Desperation gripped him in the last moments of clarity. He logged into his server at home via his phone, queued up his favorite playlist and renamed it "Little Wind."

26.

How do you know who to trust when everyone lies?
— Random Thought # 490

∿

Waking up from a drug-induced stupor was starting
to feel almost normal to Elms. At least, normal in
the sense that the last few times she woke were all
through a chemical haze.

Light streamed through the mini blinds that
covered the only window of her private hospital
room and bathed the room in clean light. Pure
energy all on a single beam of sunlight. It plucked a
chord in her heart and warmed her through and
through.

"She lives." The words dripped with

sarcasm.

Elms rolled over and was met by the beautiful face of a stranger. "I'm sorry, do I know you?"

"I'm sure Simon's mentioned me." The woman's smile did little to mask the cruel glint in her eye.

"Simon?" The name sounded familiar, but she couldn't put a face to it.

"You know. The guy you tried to lure away from his rightful mate." The pretense of a smile disappeared.

"I have no idea what you are talking about," she whispered dumbfounded.

"Stop lying, bitch. I know what you did. He's supposed to be with Tiffy. So leave him alone. I know he'll try to come here and fix things with you, but you need to let him go. What you're doing is killing Tiffy, and hurting him, too, only he's too infatuated by you to see the truth."

Elms searched the woman's face for indications of falsehoods and deceptions, but none existed. Then it dawned on her, the man who had barged into her room a couple nights ago in the ICU. She was pretty sure his name had been Simon. He'd wanted to talk to her, but he hadn't said anything about them being an item.

"I'm sorry. I was in an accident and the doctors say that my memory might take a while to come back. If I did something to upset you, I'm truly sorry." Elms struggled to sit upright in bed to face her accuser.

234

"Whatever. Just stay away from my brother. By the end of next week, he and Tiffy'll be bonded, and then I can get on with finding my Tiffy."

A look flashed across her face but disappeared before Elms could let it sink in.

"Stay away. Got it?"

Elms nodded and watched the stranger leave as quietly as she had come.

A few hours later, Elms sat in bed watching trashy TV. The doctor and his team of ducklings had already come by and given her an update on her progress. They had little to offer about the state of her memory, but they were optimistic that she'd be discharged before the end of the day.

By early afternoon she was bored. Sue called and offered to come sit with her, but Elms refused. It'd be soon enough that she'd be calling Sue for a ride home. Her phone was probably still in the truck, so she asked her aunt to call Sophie and ask for time off while she healed and regained her memory.

She was surprised Sophie hadn't come in to see her yet. It wasn't like her not to visit community clients when they were at the human hospital. A nagging sensation tugged at eh back of her brain, but she couldn't make it stop vibrating in her mind long enough to make it hold still.

She flipped through the channels and drummed her fingers on the tray table across her lap. A soft knock at the door sounded.

"Come in," she called, and was rewarded

with a huge teddy bear that peeked around the door first, followed by Colin. Colin being the man who'd kissed her last night, if she could trust her memory. But something seemed to be blocking the memories following it. She had wondered all morning if he would come so she could ask him directly to fill in the gaps.

"Delivery for a Ms. Elma McMillan." He pitched his all-too distinct voice in a falsetto.

"Hey, Colin, right? Come in. I'm glad you came. Did you hear that I might be sprung this afternoon?" She eyed the huge bear in his arms and the shy look on his face.

He nodded his head and a shy smile caressed his lips. "Yeah. Sue mentioned it. I stopped by and got you a bag of stuff, in case they did give you the boot."

Her favorite pink and silver plaid overnight bag slid from his shoulder and dropped at the foot of the bed.

"Yay." She reached for the bag, her head landing a mere few inches from Colin's crotch, and panicked. This had to look downright scandalous to anyone who might walk in. Heat colored her cheeks as she retreated with the bag and sat back in bed. "Sorry about that."

Colin's face reddened. "El, we gotta talk." He shifted the bear in his arms and looked unsure what to do with it.

"That for me?"

Relief swamped his face. "Yeah. Picked him up before I heard you might be home tonight. I didn't wantcha here all by your lonesome for another night." He handed the stuffed animal over. It was almost as big as she was.

"Thanks." She hugged it to her chest. "So, are you going to tell me what's been going on? I've noticed some definite changes." Her blush resurfaced and heat spread through her body. "I can't remember specifics," she finished. The color that had stained his cheeks was fading. Bingo. He was finally the person who could fill in her blanks, she could feel it.

"Why don't you tell me what you do remember, and I'll do the best I can to fill in the rest." He dragged a chair to the side of her bed and sat, hands perched on his knees, anticipation in his eyes.

"Well, I…" She ducked behind the bear for cover. "I have these memories that are like a movie with a hole in the film. I can see myself and a man in the woods out by the reservoir." She peered around the broad head of the fluff she clutched. Colin didn't flinch, but he didn't meet her eyes either.

"What do you remember happening in the woods, El?"

She ducked back behind the bear and mentally eenie-meenied her answer. If she wanted the truth from him, she'd have to be honest, too.

"I'm pretty sure we had sex." Heat flashed through her like a memory all of its own and scorched a path from her heart to her girly bits. When Colin didn't say anything, she moved the bear and searched his face. His knuckles were white and his full lips were drawn into a tight colorless line. "Colin? You can tell me if I overstepped and we took something too far."

"Why'd you say that?"

His voice strained and she could see the tenuous strand of control he was grasping.

"Why would it've been you who overstepped, El? Are you so certain it wasn't..." His words stopped and his eyes turned cold. His knuckles cracked under the pressure forced on them against his legs.

"You're scaring me." Her voice betrayed her and she shook like a leaf in a wind storm. "I mean the way you kissed me last night, I thought we'd maybe gotten together. Dec mentioned something about a date with you, and I just thought..."

His voice rose and the deep rumble of it rolled over her like thunder. "I kissed you because I thought I had lost you. Did you know how worried I was when you wouldn't answer your phone Friday night? One minute you were dancing, and the next you were gone. I'd called and called, and you never answered.

"I thought I had pushed you too far. I thought you'd run from me, but it wasn't me you were running from, was it, El? You were running to *him*." His icy gaze burned her. "Was that why you've been so weird lately? You were too busy playing around with that Fire? That asshole who'd supposed to marry Tiffy? What the hell were you thinking?"

Her stomach clenched and then the locked doors in her head sprang open. Memory after memory suffocated her and overwhelmed her senses. Eyes blue as the ocean burned with fire behind them. The glint of a diamond stud earring. The heat coursing through her body at the slightest touch. The thrill of feeling him tucked deep within her body. The shudder of pleasure as he whispered 'Little Wind' in her ear right before he climaxed. A climax that was brighter than fireworks, but didn't burn her skin. Good Goddess. She could still feel her body quaking with the pleasure at the memory of his goatee tickling between her legs. A moan slipped through her lips and she was yanked back to the present by the sound of metal scraping across linoleum.

Colin towered over her, a scowl on his face. "I don't think I want to know what just happened." He shook his head.

"Knock, knock," a nurse sing-songed, as she walked in. The woman eyed Colin and bit her bottom lip, and then moved to Elms. "Are we ready to go home? I have all your paperwork here, so all we need to do is get you unhooked from this IV and go over a few things. Then you're free to go."

Her smile should've been contagious, but Elms couldn't muster one to return. Colin leaned against the far wall and studied her while the nurse set to work disconnecting the IV and went over all the doctor's discharge instructions, including a follow-up appointment in his main office that Elms had no plans to keep.

"Will you need some help getting dressed, or will your fellow be able to help?" The nurse winked in her direction and waited until Elms shook her head 'no' before retreating from the room. "Just give me a holler when you're ready, and I'll get transport up here to wheel you out. 'Kay?"

"Okay," she called.

Colin met her eyes, a challenge evident in his look. She shifted to the edge of the bed and sat up all on her own. Step one complete. Now all she had to do was manage to dress herself without needing his help. She opened the overnight bag and looked at the options before her. Not a single pair of yoga pants or a big comfy t-shirt to be found. Instead, she found a matching lingerie set with pale pink roses embroidered on delicate ivory silk, a pair of white leggings and a sweater dress that still had the tags on it. It was the same sky blue as her eyes and was softer than the silk of the lacy underthings.

She raised a brow in question at Colin. "Where did all this come from?"

He stuffed his hands in his pockets and found a speck of dirt on the floor specifically appealing. "I asked your aunt for your sizes. I wanted to do something nice to make up for whatever I did the other night to send you away." Emotion clouded his every syllable. "What does he have that I don't, El? Just tell me and I will get it for you."

"Oh, Colin, I'm so sorry. I didn't mean to tell you all that. I thought... Well, I thought maybe it was you. The kiss..."

"You mean the kiss that almost put you into a coma? The one that ripped you in two? At first I thought you were having pain from the accident, but you weren't, were you? It was him. Always fucking him. He did that to you." He shoved away from the wall he'd been leaning and paced around the small room like a heavy weight champ ready to fight. "He can't have you, El. You aren't Fire and he isn't Wind. Besides, when I saw him yesterday, he seemed pleased as pie to be arranging his bonding ceremony." He eyed her with a look that was purely meant to sting, and it landed with a jolt. "Tiffy's parents have already started the ball rolling. Friday the whole fucking town is invited to watch their daughter say I do. *To him.*"

"No." The gasp escaped before she could stop it.

Colin had to be wrong. Every memory of Simon was full of whispered promises. Ones his body made to hers while he'd played her like a fine violin. He'd stroked her into the belief that life without him would be forever lacking. That the fire he could give her was something she needed to live almost as much as she needed air in her lungs.

Crap. Her face fell as more memories swirled around her. Simon naked in the shower, water washing away the bliss they had shared and replacing it with a sense of duty and obligation. Oh, Goddess. She remembered. He'd said goodbye, and she'd left him without putting up a fight.

The kiss with Colin last night had sealed it. Whatever joke Fate played with her emotions was becoming crystal clear in her head. The kiss had begun the split. The split of the bond she hadn't known was forming. The bond between her and Simon.

Tears poured from her eyes. This was her destiny. Just like her mentor. Being a healer was so all-encompassing that it took everything the healer had, so Fate gave them an out in love. An out she never wanted. Even though she hadn't been looking for her mate, for Simon, she'd known that someday she'd want him.

Something similar had happened to Sophie. She'd gotten married to a human to the displeasure of the council. A human who'd loved her the best he could. A human who'd unknowingly provided her with a half-breed child. A human who'd lost his sanity when he learned that Sophie was an Elemental, and that the new town he'd moved her to, was the home of Sophie's fated mate. Sophie had begged her husband to believe that she had chosen him above the ways of her culture, but he couldn't let it go. In a horrific clash of ideals, Sophie consciously broke her bond with Isaac Strom, the current town elder and her fated mate, and offered her heart to her husband, Joseph George. But it hadn't been enough. Fate won out in the vicious game of tug of war over Sophie's full devotion. Isaac and she were close to this day, but they couldn't fix the irreparable broken bond, and Joseph had to be spelled by a local coven of witches to keep him from coming after Sophie and her daughter Gracelynn. Now Elms was looking at a similar future, but without the daughter to keep her company.

Selfish as it was, she reached a hand to Colin and pulled herself into his warm embrace. She would live the rest of this lifetime alone and without the comfort of a man, if she was right about what had happened last night. Colin's embrace soothed her pain, but ignited an unchained desire that churned like acid in her gut and chipped away the potential to ever feel uninhibited and free again. She knew it was wrong, but she needed to feel alive one more time before she gave in to the solitude of her future, so she threaded her hands into his hair and pulled until their lips were separated by only a breath.

Throwing caution out the window, she closed the gap.

27.

Hit rewind and play it again, Jack.
- Random Thought # 975

∿

Being held hostage by a doting aunt, an overbearing friend, and a couch that sunk in the middle to the point of needing a prize-winning strong man to get her out was getting old by the time Friday rolled around. Her head no longer beat in time with her heart and her limbs only showed yellow traces of the bruises she'd sustained in the accident. Too bad her legs still threatened to buckle if she stood or, Goddess forbid, wanted to walk on them.

Every chance she got, she looked out the huge bay window in the living room in the hope that she'd find JT's tow truck coming down the road with her uncle's truck rigged on the back. That and her cell phone. Snow had fallen Monday afternoon during her ride home from the hospital and gone on for a few days. The roads were passable now, thanks to the plows and brine trucks that had been up and down the main and secondary arteries over the last twenty-four hours, so she didn't feel quite so guilty about one of JT's guys being out on the road.

"Are you ready for some lunch?" Her aunt smiled and set a tray on the coffee table.

Two huge bowls of baked potato soup with all the fixings caught her eye and made her mouth water. "Yum. I'd love some soup. Thanks."

"Let me help you sit up," Sue offered.

"I'll get her," Colin piped up from her uncle's favorite recliner.

"I can do it myself," she growled.

Since the moment she had gotten home, Colin had been bunking in her aunt's guest room. Every morning he insisted on helping her down the stairs to the couch, every meal he insisted on helping lift her to a sitting position, and every evening he insisted on tucking her into bed. Every time she argued, he shrugged and ignored her. This time was about to be the first exception, so she swung her legs over the edge of the couch and aimed for a controlled fall onto the living room floor when her feet refused to cooperate.

"Why didn'tcha wait?" His hands slid under her armpits.

"Because I can do it myself."

Her tone was more like a cranky four-year-old than a grown woman, but she wasn't about to let someone do one more thing for her; above all, Colin. She appreciated his dedication to her recovery, but the way he looked at her, like he was just waiting for her to fall at his feet and profess her undying love was too much to handle.

She twisted out of his reach and used the coffee table for leverage. When her feet planted beneath her and her legs didn't buckle, she gave him her best 'told you so' look and took a cautious step toward the dining room. If her legs had felt steadier, she would've aimed for the kitchen table, but the dining room would serve as a good compromise between success and failure, despite the fact that the weakness would surely taunt her later.

"I'll get the tray," Sue called, her smile evident in her tone of voice.

Earlier in the week she voiced concern about letting Colin stay and be so 'helpful,' but Elms wasn't ready to deal with the guilt of kicking him out. First, the weather had been atrocious and, second, she had practically invited his attention with that stunt she pulled in the hospital.

Elms felt Colin at her elbow but ignored him and continued her slow steps. The crunch of tires on snow turned her attention back toward the front window.

"Finally. He's here." She pushed through the pain and limped to the front door.

"Who's here, dear?"

"JT. He's got Iggy's truck which means I'll finally have my cell back." She opened the door, gripping it harder than usual to offset the shift of her weight when it swung wide.

"Hey, Crash," called JT's lead mechanic and son, Jared.

"About time you got it all fixed, Jar. What took so long?"

"Besides everything? You did a hell of a number on the old girl."

She watched him work the levers for the pneumatic lift, his biceps bulging under his thermal shirt.

When the truck was on solid ground, he smiled at her. "So whatcha so eager 'bout anyway? I thought your Jeep's working. Unless you decided to drive that off a cliff, too." His eyes twinkled with laughter.

"Real funny, Jar. Hey, do you have the bag with all my stuff in it? Your dad said he'd have it delivered with the truck."

He nodded, reached in the cab of his rig, and pulled a paper grocery bag from the A & P from the truck's floorboard. "Got it right here." His boots left footprints in the fresh snow when he tromped up the front steps. He handed her the keys and brown bag. "All kidding aside, are you okay, Elms? Rumor has it you had a mental breakdown or something."

His curious gaze pierced her heart. Is that what people really thought? That she'd lost her mind and driven off a cliff? She supposed it made sense, since she didn't shift before impact, but it had happened too quick. The thought hadn't entered her mind until she was already bruised and battered. The short and long of it was that she had had an airhead moment; one where she did something irrevocably stupid.

"No mental breakdown or anything. I got preoccupied with my phone." She shrugged. "All those bumper stickers are right. Texting while driving is dangerous."

"Well, I'm glad to see you up and around." He tipped his ball cap in salute and waded through the powder back to the flatbed.

She watched him U-turn and head back to the main road.

"You should come inside so you don't catch a cold." The ice in Colin's voice was colder than the temperature outside.

"In a minute." She despised her weakness. She clutched the bag in her hand and willed her body to cooperate when she marched, albeit slowly, back to the dining room. She slumped in the chair and a whoosh of air evacuated her lungs like a deflating Macy's parade balloon.

She took a cautious spoonful of the soup and thanked her lucky stars that Sue was cooking. Her aunt had the culinary skills of an Amish grandma, unlike Colin. If she would've been stuck at home with him as her sole caretaker there'd be a good chance she'd have starved by now.

She set the soup aside to let it cool and

riffled through the bag Jared had brought. At the very bottom was her purse, and at the very bottom of it was her phone. Her dead phone. She eased the chair back and made her way to the stairs. From the bottom they looked like Mt. Vesuvius, complete with lava flow.

"El, whatcha need? I can get it for you."

"I can do it myself, thanks."

The bite of sarcasm was all it took to call Colin off. He was helpful, no doubt about it, but it was time she stood on her own. She took the first step and held on to the railing with all her strength. She felt like a mountain climber as she struggled up the stairs. By the time she hit the top landing, she felt invincible. Sore and breathless, but invincible. She shuffled to her room, fingertips grazing the wall in case she needed it for support, then plopped on her bed. She slid the cord for the wall charger off her nightstand and clicked it into place on her phone.

The minutes ticked by slower than her ascent up the freakin' stairs, until finally a red light signaled that her resuscitation efforts worked. She pressed the on button and waited while the screen flickered to life. The ticker of text messages blinked before her eyes until each missed message had registered. She clicked into the phone section of the device and viewed the list of missed calls. A bunch from Colin on Friday night and Saturday morning, one from Sophie timed right around the time she left a message on the office line, and one from Tiffy. That one had a voice mail attached. She clicked over to the voicemail system and listened.

"Elma. Where the hell are you? Something's wrong. I can't be fated for Dilbert guy because I'm pretty sure I'm hot for his sister. Where are you? Shit. Call me as soon as you get this."

At once, it all made sense. Tiffy's exploding. Her frustration. Her desire to not have to bond. She had a secret that the community wouldn't want to accept. Elms needed to find Simon, to find her slice of happiness, and to stop Tiffy from marrying him to keep the peace.

Strength Elms didn't know she possessed launched her off the bed and out the door. The doorframe dug into her palms when her balance faltered. Her knees buckled beneath her, wobbling like gelatin had been shaped into bone-like tubes and implanted in the flesh of her legs. The crack of her shoulder against the doorframe echoed down the stairs.

"El, what's going on?" Colin mounted the steps, one heavy footfall at a time, slowed by her earlier rebuff. "I'm coming…"

"I'm fine." It was a lie he could disprove all to soon once he rounded the corner—unless he didn't. Then it was a lie she could live with. She gritted her teeth against the pain screaming in her lower extremities and righted. The steps to the top of the stairs undid her, she would regret every one of them. Colin froze midway, eyes full of incredulity, disbelief, accusation. "Don't look at me like that." She shook the nausea nagging her nervous system away with a hard shake of her head.

"Whatcha doing?"

"None of your business." Defiance colored every syllable.

"El..."

"Don't start with me." She limped down the stairs, imagined her eyes slicing deep into the blockade that was her friend, then grunted at him when he didn't move.

"Let me help." The brush of his hand on her arm was enough to make her anger ratchet up a notch or two.

"If you want to keep that hand, keep it away from me."

She dared not swat at him with the questionable cease-fire between her and balance at the moment. She wasn't being fair and she knew it, but he would stop her and she couldn't let that happen. He retreated to the living room in a huff and guilt washed over her with the gentleness of a piece of steel wool.

The front door loomed ahead. All she needed was ten normal paces to lift her over the threshold. She swallowed her pain, guilt, and last shred of sanity, all with the finesse of a novice sword swallower.

She slipped her purse from the clothes tree by the door and jangled her keys free.

"Elma, where do you think you are going?"

"Out. I'll be back soon. There's something I have to do."

"But you aren't wearing proper shoes."

"I'll be fine, Aunt Sue."

Her unicorn slippers hadn't failed her yet
and she had faith they wouldn't now. She eased
herself down the front steps. The cold seeped
through the plush white fabric of her slippers when
her feet sunk below the surface layer of snow. The
gold twisted horns stood proud above the snow
cover, a beacon that led the way to her Jeep. The
door opened and closed behind her, the weight of
boots thundered on the porch.

"Let me drive you. Wherever you want to
go." A plea was laced through Colin's words.
"Don't be stubborn, it's not like you."

"Maybe it is, Colin." The crunch of his
boots in the snow taunted her. "I'm going to see
Simon."

"El." That one syllable said it all. It carried
his distrust, disgust, displeasure, and distress. So
much weight behind one little word.

"You can't stop me." She carried on, the
truck getting closer with each freezing step.

"But I know where he is."

His words registered enough to halt her
forward momentum. "Where?"

"Let me drive you."

"No."

"Look, I know you think you have
something with this guy, and if it takes you seeing
him with someone else to make you see how wrong
you are, I'll do it." His footsteps sank beside her
shivering unicorns. "Come on, El."

"Fine."

One word was all the permission Colin

needed because he hefted her off her feet and
carried her to his snow-covered truck. After
depositing her in the passenger seat and turning
over the engine to warm the truck, he went to work
clearing the snow from the hood, windshield, and
bed cover. When he slid into the driver's seat,
flakes of snow clung to his hair like fleas on a dog.
The image ripped a giggle from her throat.

"What?"

"Nothing." She refused to share. "So, how
do you know where Simon is?"

"Tomorrow's the wedding, El. Tonight's the
rehearsal. Most of the community's been invited to
The Tack House for a mating party."

His words stung. She sat in silence while he
drove the plowed roads toward the old Moravian
church. It was the only place where members of the
community got married. An enchantment that
deterred humans made it the safest place in all of
Harmony, Hope, and neighboring town of
Belvidere for the members of the community
congregate.

The lot had been plowed and salted from
the looks of it. Her stomach dropped at the sheer
number of vehicles in the parking lot. Her eye
found Simon's sleek little roadster beside Tiffy's
pickup and her heart plummeted. A strangled cry
lodged in her throat.

"El…"

"Don't. It's not gonna happen. I know it."
"You need to accept it."

She could feel his eyes judging her every

movement, every intake of breath, every blink of her lashes. She held back the tears that threatened to spill with every fiber of her being.

"He won't go through with it." The whispered words were a plea to the ether as much as they were a conviction she needed to hear aloud to believe.

"Why not? He's come this far. And he hasn't come looking for you."

The truth in his words hit home and shattered a piece of her soul in the process. The tears trickled over her lids and down her cheeks. She swiped them away and straightened her sweatshirt. Oh, Goddess, what had she been thinking? She was in her most comfy old sweatpants and one of Declan's Earth, Wind, & Fire sweatshirts; the band was comprised of a bunch of Elementals. And here she was to win back the man she loved wearing a joke. She pulled the rearview mirror and took a hard look at herself. Nothing about her looked put together or sane, but it was now or never. She had enough guilt about interrupting his wedding rehearsal, but the actual wedding was something she didn't think she could bring herself to do.

"You don't have to go in there. I'll take you back home. All you have to do is say the word."

The hurt in Colin's eyes was evident. She hated to do this to him, after she had so carelessly played with his heart, but she had to talk to Simon even if he only told her to go away.

The huge church door hinges protested like

they knew what she was about to do—it didn't stop her. When Isaac Strom stopped mid-sentence during the rehearsal service—it didn't stop her. When everyone in the room turned to watch her limp down the aisle—it didn't stop her. Nothing could make her weak legs stop their forward motion until she stood directly in front of the only man who'd ever made her burn and want more from life than to be a success in the eyes of the community. The man who had shown her what love was wore confusion like a Mardi Gras mask. His aura a troubling array of colors, but the most troubling of all was the dark grey overlay that hovered like a scar directly over his heart. Even that didn't stop her.

"Oh, Fire Guy, what've you done?"

28.

Smile and nod until they think you're okay. –
Random Thought # 19

~~

The tiny redhead standing chest height before him
looked like someone had done a number on her.
Her long hair was tangled and the shirt she wore
was at least three sizes too big. But her eyes; they
spoke to him. He got lost in the bluest blue he'd
ever seen, so clear and deep like the crystal clear
waters surrounding a tropical island. The pained
look on her face tugged at the broken strands of
memories he no longer could grasp. Unsure how to
proceed with her, he smiled and waited.

"Simon, can we talk?" Her voice was soft

and chimed like bells.

He looked around the church, all eyes on the woman before him, and shrugged. "Sure, why not?" He followed her uneven gait to the back of the church. "How can I help you?"

"I needed to talk to you before you married Tiffy. I'm so sorry about what happened at the hospital. The accident caused some memory loss, but it's better now."

He could see a proverbial cloud hanging over her as she waited for him to say something. Anything would do, he realized, as the silence stretched on between them.

"I don't know what you're talking about."

Her face crumpled at his honesty and he could barely suppress the urge to reach out and console the stranger with an embrace.

"Simon, do you remember me? We met a couple of weeks ago?"

"I'm sorry. I can't place your face."

"Do you remember the first night you met Tiffy? The exploding? And then we met in the parking lot. Remember?"

Her expectant look pierced his heart. "I'm sorry. I don't."

"How about the reservoir? I dumped you in it? Remember that?"

"Shit. I must've done something pretty terrible for you to dump me in a reservoir. Sorry."

"No. Actually, you kinda flamed out. You really don't remember?" Her shoulders slumped and her voice faltered.

Goddess, this little thing was trying to tell him something important, but for the life of him, he couldn't begin to decipher the meaning behind her words. Was she angry that he'd lost his temper? That was usually his reason for bursting out in flame. Either that or she'd piqued his interest. He cocked his head and took in every inch of her petite physique. That might've been it. She was adorable. Even under the baggy clothes he could see that she had a great figure. He felt a familiar rush of heat spark through his body. It had been a long time since he'd been so affected by a woman. He met her eyes again only to find tears simmering at the corner of her lids.

"No, but I'm not surprised. I woke up a few days ago in the hospital with an empty bottle of 'forget.' I figured something must've happened that I needed a rewind on. My dad's an elder, so I know a witch's potion when I see one." It still wasn't clear why he'd taken the potion. His sister refused to have any knowledge of him even taking it, which he still found odd. But since he'd woken, he'd noticed that he and Shiv seemed to no longer share the connection they'd been born with. She reassured him that it was because of him meeting his mate, and he had no reason not to trust her.

"Oh, Simon. Why? Why would you take that? Don't you know what it does?" She looked around the church and lowered her lashes.

"Pretty sure I remember my dad telling us, it's like a rewind button. It packs some steep consequences, but I can't imagine I'd take it lightly.

Besides, whatever my reasons were, life seems to be turning out okay. I'm marrying my mate tomorrow. My parents are on their way in, and I think Tiffany's parents have invited everyone in the area. Will you be there?" Something about her called to a part of him he forgot ever existed and in spite of his looming nuptials, he needed to know if the redhead would be there. Even if it was so that he could see her one more time before leaving town. The thought shook him to the core.

"No. I'm pretty sure no one would want me there."

Her words clawed at him. How could someone so delicate look so broken? "Why?"

"Well, it might have something to do with the fact that I was Tiffy's healer and I let myself get involved with you."

"Involved? How so?" A flash of something blinked across her face and his heart skipped a beat. *Involved*, involved? Huh.

"This was a huge mistake."

"What the fuck do you think you're doing? I thought I made it clear that you needed to stay away from my brother." His sister, a hurricane of emotion, invaded their space and separated them.

"Shiv, it's okay. We're just talking."

"Si, you can't talk to her. It'll hurt Tiffy. You don't remember, but you wandered off from Tiffy before with this woman and it nearly destroyed her."

Before he could formulate a response, the redhead was on her tiptoes in his sister's face.

"It wasn't because Simon wandered off. Go ask Tiffy if you don't believe me."

"You're lying." The words hung thick with accusation between the women. "Tiffy was an intrinsic component in helping Simon recover the memories that you took from him. Don't think I don't know that you dosed him with the stuff that made him forget Tiffy. You could've ruined everything, you bitch."

"Shiv," he warned, but the sprite of a woman backed down. Sadness pulled at her lips and his heart warred with his brain to find a something that could replace that frown with a smile.

"It's okay Simon. I was wrong to come here."

The stranger stood on her tiptoes in soggy bedroom slippers that looked like droopy unicorns. Could that be right? Unicorns? Before he could contemplate it further, she ran her hand down his chest, placed a heated kiss on his lips, and was gone in a gust of wind the color of crushed pearls. Ah, she was a Wind... It was only then that it occurred to him, he never got the Little Wind's name.

The rest of the afternoon was a whirlwind of activity. Simon looked around the private room at The Tack Room and took in the vast number of people who had shown up to celebrate Tiffy's mating. The best part was that besides his sister,

Isaac, and his soon-to-be-family, he didn't know anyone else in the room. And the people he did know were practically strangers with the exception of his twin.

The forget potion was strong, he'd give the witch that made it that much, but it wasn't as strong as some potions he'd heard of over the years. When he'd woken up, he'd known who he was and he remembered most of his life in general. But why he was in this Podunk town in the middle of nowhere alluded him. He was lucky he had taken the potion while his phone was on him, because Siobhan had been quick to fill him in on the pertinent information.

In the last week, he'd spent more time planning a mating than he thought was possible for one man to do. Tiffy wasn't so bad, as far as mates went, but every time she got stressed, her voice would hit a pitch that reminded him of nails on a chalkboard. Cringe-inducing as it was, he looked forward to getting past the actual ceremony and connecting in the way of their people. Although, it did bother him that up until now he still didn't feel compelled to be near her, to hold her, to invade her. The possessiveness he expected was missing. He watched his mate stalk from one guest to the next.

Tiffy shot him a sidelong glance that was as empty as his memories of their earlier courting. He wanted to ask her about it, but something gnawed at the back of his mind. The kiss the Wind had given him in the church was meant as a goodbye, that much he could tell. It had been there in every beat of his heart in the brief time it took, but for the life of him, he couldn't figure out why she'd be saying goodbye. Especially now that snippets of flaming red hair were dancing through his mind over and over and over again. The memories tickled the recesses of his brain while people moved around him on fast forward. Humans had rehearsal dinners, which was the easiest thing to equate a mating party to, but in their custom the bride and groom didn't interact much the night before the ceremony that would bind them for life. In fact, it was quite the opposite. The community went out of their way to keep the mating pair separate.

"You ready to head out?"

It wasn't until Shiv plopped down beside him that he realized the mating party was wrapping up.

"Almost." He turned to meet her eyes. "So what was all that earlier?"

"What?"

"With the Wind? You know what she wanted, don't you?"

"Oh, Si." She wound her arm through his and pulled him toward the door. "She's a troublemaker. She almost came between you and Tiffy. I told her to leave you alone, but apparently she didn't get the message, since she was at the church this afternoon. Put her out of your mind and focus on tomorrow." They walked out into the chill of the evening.

"I keep having these flashes. Like memories.

But different."

"You almost fucked up your mating. Maybe it's your guilty conscience smacking you upside the head for allowing her to interrupt today."

He pulled Siobhan into a dark corner. "Wait. That was real?" He shook his head to stave off the onslaught of memories. "Holy shit! I took her virginity in the woods." The images raced through his head faster than an empty express train at midnight.

"You what?" Shiv's mouth dropped wide. "Oh, Si. Tell me you didn't."

He didn't need their twin connection to see the disappointment etched on her face.

"I need a drink." He swung around to the front of The Tack House, only to find the manager locking up behind the stranglers of their party. Memories of The Outpost parking lot sprang to mind and Elms; that was his Wind's name. She sprang into every thought. Ethereal in nothing but an afghan and the same unicorn slippers that she had worn down the aisle of the church today. He remembered. His keys materialized in his hand while his boots crunched across the salt-covered asphalt.

"Where are you going?"

He could hear his sister's steps chasing his and worry haunted her voice.

"To get that drink. Are you coming?" He didn't wait for her answer. He was in the car and shifting into drive when his sister swung the passenger door open.

"Where to?"

"The only place that'll be open this late in no-man's land."

29.

If stupidity is contagious get me a mask 'cause I've already got a raging case of the stupids. - Random Thought # 37

∿

Fire burned Elms' trachea in the wake of the whiskey. Her slippers were finally dry and, thanks to Eddie, she was wrapped in an Outpost long-sleeved tee instead of Dec's sweatshirt. It wasn't much of an improvement overall, but Elms had gotten lucky when she'd stumbled into the only place that wouldn't judge her for drinking herself senseless. Dec, Charlie, and Maureen had all been nursing a pitcher of beer when she'd gimped her way into the bar before dinner. Thankfully,

Maureen had taken pity on her and leant her a hairbrush and some lip gloss. At least now she wasn't the picture of crazy.

She was, however, the picture of drunk. Elms leaned a little too much on the bar for support, and her voice was loud even to her own ears. The weight of Colin's stare could be felt on her back. His disapproval was evident when she told him to leave her there when they'd first walked in, and it wasn't getting any better with each gulp she swallowed down. Why he hadn't left baffled her. She could find her own way home, but he'd insisted on staying. Even after Declan and Charlie had both separately promised to ensure she arrived home safe and sound, he'd insisted on staying put. Too bad he was oblivious to the fact that his insistence was grating on her very last, overly raw nerve.

She shook the weight of his stare off and tossed the remnants of her whiskey back. Her phone sat lifeless on the bar beside her. She should've charged it longer before rushing off to throw herself at someone else's man, then she could play one of the many boredom busting games she had to her name.

"Another Eddie?"

"Ah, Elms, are yuh sure? 'S not like yuh."

"It's been one of those days, Eddie. And tomorrow's not gonna be any better, so the more I drink now, the less I'll be awake tomorrow to drown in my own stupidity. I should've known I wouldn't be able to handle my first solo case."

Eddie's wife sidled next to him, "When's Ms. Sophie back, Elms?"

"Hey, Janice. Soon. She left me a message the other day. Sounds like Gracie finally came into her gifts. Something about it being unexpected." The matching shock on their faces forced her to shut her lips.

"I thought she was a halfie and they don't get gifts." Prejudice colored every word leaking from Janice's mouth and they hung midair ripening with each passing second.

"Uh, nature calls." Elms stumbled off the barstool and limped to the restrooms. She needed to get a grip before she started spewing secrets left and right about community members who would be all to happy to see her stoned old-school witch-style if she let loose the wrong ones.

"El, you okay?"

"I just have to use the little girl's room, Colin. I'll be right back, I'm not leaving." Regret filled her the moment the words left her mouth and it mounted when his aura shifted from concern to hurt. His abandonment issues were one of the many secrets she held and she'd thrown it in his face. Why? Because he cared enough to stay well past ten while she drank herself into oblivion? Because he cared enough to worry while she stumbled toward the dark hallway of the bar? Or was it because she knew he loved her and she would never be able to love him back?

Tears clouded her vision, so she did what she did best. She ran. At least that's what she attempted on her cursed legs. She pushed past him with her stilted gait until the stall door locked behind her. The more she cried, the more her stomach rebelled, and the more her stomach churned, the more the whiskey burned her throat as it threatened to spew into the commode. She finally gave up the fight and let it loose. She deserved the pain, the embarrassment, the wretchedness of it all. She'd played with fire and gotten burned. And this burn would last for the rest of her life.

When her stomach felt as empty as her heart, she faced the stranger in the mirror and splashed water on her face. Colin was sitting alone at the table where her cousin and his friends had been. Disgust simmered through his aura. An icy glare wasn't targeted on her, though. She followed the freeze-rays from his eyes and saw the one person she would give anything to see. Simon. He and his sister were huddled at a table by the door.

She swallowed back the indecision that gripped her and made her way back to the barstool. If Simon was here, it sure wasn't to talk to her. He'd taken the Forget knowing full well that he'd lose memories of her, she was sure of it. So there was no reason for her to throw herself at his feet again, just to be humiliated one more time. Instead, she flagged Eddie down and ordered a hot tea.

"Can I join you, Elms?"

"It's a free country, but won't your sister have a problem?" She nodded toward his sister at the corner of the bar in a conversation with Janice.

"She'll get over it."

"Doubtful. So you remembered my name?"

Silence descended on them when Janice brought over the tea and a beer for Simon. The accusation in her eyes told her that Siobhan had already told the woman every little secret she knew about Elms and Simon.

"Thanks to that kiss earlier, I seem to be remembering a whole lot of things."

A blush warmed her face and Simon's familiar warmth seeped through her veins. "I'm sure it's nothing worth mentioning," she edged and sipped her tea.

The liquid coated her tongue in an unfamiliar burst of heat mixed with sweetness. Eddie must be branching out from the traditional Lipton he usually kept in stock; probably was Janice's influence. Ever since the two had mated, she'd been busy adding her touch to all aspects of the bar's business.

"You wanted to talk earlier and now you won't even look at me."

She swung around and glared at him, the strange flavor inundating her senses. "Look, you're marrying Tiffy. You made it clear that you wanted to mate within your class and I respect that. But just so you know, Tiffy knows you're not her mate. She left me a message saying as much. So the two of you are just kidding yourselves with all this." His face clouded over and she looked away to avoid the shifting colors of his aura that gave him away and took another swallow of the tea. "Fate crapped all over me starting the morning of my thirteenth birthday. She gave me a gift that makes me vomit, a mate that isn't in my class, a life I'll always want but can never have. Besides that, what else could there be to discuss? Unless something's changed between you and Tiffy."

The whoosh of his breath made it clear that nothing had changed. "It's okay, Simon. I get it. You're a Fire. I'm a Wind. The two don't mix. Whatever." With the last of her bravado fading, she hopped off the stool and made her way through the bar to her ever-present friend, bodyguard, jailor, shoulder to cry on.

"Let's get out of here."

"Where to?"

The question was a barely concealed growl which meant Colin had witnessed the exchange between her and Simon. She pulled her bottom lip between her teeth. "How much of that did you hear?"

Colin's ears glowed red. He stood and shoved his hands in the pockets of his jeans.

"So all of it?"

"El." He wrapped his hand around her arm and gently pulled her toward the door.

"No, it's okay."

Once they were outside, he stopped her forward momentum and laid his hands on her shoulders. "I know you think Fate made this happen, but can'tya see that maybe you're wrong? Winds mate with Winds and if you'll give me half a chance..."

"I'm sorry. I can't." She shrugged out of his

embrace. "I'm not wrong about Simon. But even though I know that won't ever work, I don't think I could string you along either. It wouldn't be fair to either of us."

Colin raised his hands, "Okay. I'll back off, but if you change your mind, all you have to do is say so. 'Kay?"

"Thanks."

Her slippers squished in the snow, wet again. She climbed into the cab of Colin's truck and laid back against the seat, her body trembling. The confrontation with Simon was too much for her healing body. She reached for the seatbelt and missed.

"Need help?"

"Yeah. Too much whiskey, drama, everything." The words slurred out of a mouth that was too heavy to move.

The alcohol shouldn't be affecting her like this now. Colin reached over to grab the seatbelt, his hand brushing her breast as he lowered the clip into the buckle on the seat. The brief contact sent her pulse racing and heat burning in her chest. She grabbed his hand and tried to focus on the outline of it, but her vision was blurring rapidly. Panic chased the bile that churned in her stomach.

No. This wasn't happening. This wasn't the whiskey, or the stress, or Simon. This was azalea. Flame azalea to be exact. And if she didn't get to Simon quickly, she was going to die.

"Colin. I need you to get Simon. Now. I think I've been poisoned." The words were a jumbled mess of consonant sounds.

"El, are you okay?" Concern clouded every corner of his handsome face. He brushed a hand over her forehead. "Goddess, El, you're burnin' up."

She tried to make her mouth form any words possible, but nothing came out.

"Hold on, El. I'll get you to the hospital."

She swung her head from side to side to tell him 'no', but he was already pulling onto the main road, taking her away from the one Fire who might care about her enough to burn the poison out of her system.

This time around, Elms was completely aware of her surroundings when she was wheeled into the Emergency Department of the hospital in Phillipsburg. Colin's wheelchair driving was as bad as his cart driving skills in the grocery store. She prayed that he wouldn't run her into people standing around at the large sign-in desk, but she was helpless to do anything about it. Her muscles were failing her as the poison took hold and her ability to move was becoming a thing of the past.

Colin barked orders at the receptionist and demanded a nurse. A reluctant triage professional gave him dirty looks when she was rudely interrupted from her intake exam of another patient. Colin's demanding and hollering achieved results, though, because Elms was wheeled back to a room almost immediately with the nurse yelling orders of her own. A needle stabbed into her tender flesh and a free run of saline poured into her veins, while another set of hands poked her other arm and siphoned blood from her veins. Words like alcohol poisoning and overdose were tossed quietly between the medical professionals. Every time someone left a side of the gurney vacant, Colin swooped in and laid a hand on what he could without disrupting the bustling hospital staff.

The beeping of the heart rate monitor gave Elms something to hold onto in the confusion of hands on her body. The room sobered when someone burst in with news that wasn't expected. Her blood alcohol level wasn't as high as anticipated, and the screening for drugs was negative. One nurse laid a hand on her cheek and begged her to tell them what she'd taken, but the fog of the poison was too much for her. The heat bubbled up and shook her body, sending the steady chirp of the machines into an erratic symphony of beeps and alarms.

"She's in a-fib. Get the paddles."

"Sir, you have to stand back."

"Clear!"

"Again."

"Clear!"

"Okay, we have sinus rhythm."

"She feels hotter than before. Let's get a new temp on her and see if her fever is spiking."

The voices cavorted around her in a clamor of commotion. Grateful for the escape, her consciousness quieted and she drifted into the abyss.

Elms woke in the silence of a private room. Sunlight was beginning to color the sky outside the window and Colin snored softly in the corner of the room on a pullout chair-bed that looked more like a torture device than a guest sleeping station. The tidal waves of heat had receded and her hands and feet now moved on demand. The room was almost identical to the one she had spent time in after the accident, but if she didn't find Simon fast, it would be the last room she ever live in.

Even though all the fluids seemed to have diluted the toxins in her blood caused by the Fire aphrodisiac, she could still feel its impact on her body. The fatigue in her muscles, the excessive saliva, the pain low in her abdomen, the bite of each breath she took. It was classic signs of azalea poisoning, and humans had no cure for it. The only way she would live through this ordeal would be to find a Fire willing to overheat her body and burn off the poison. It was risky, but her body wasn't as fragile as a human's, so the risk would be worth it. If she could find a Fire and fast.

She flung the sheet back and scooted to the edge of the bed. Grabbing onto the IV pole, she pulled herself up and shuffled to the door.

"Hon, what are you doing out of bed?" A nurse walking down the hall stopped Elms' forward momentum.

"I need to make a call." Her words didn't fail her, but the exertion it took to walk these few steps were already beginning to take a toll. She leaned against the wall for support.

"Who can I call for you?"

"Susan Price. She's my aunt." Her legs began to wobble beneath her.

The nurse nodded, carted her back to bed, then hurried down the hall. She returned with a cordless phone in hand. "Here, hon, it's ringing."

"Hello?"

Relief flooded her system just hearing her aunt's voice.

"Sue, it's Elms. I need your help. I'm at the hospital."

"What happened? Are you all right?"

"Flame azalea. In my tea. I need Simon. Please." Her hands began to tremble and the phone clattered to the floor.

"I need help over here!"

The nurse's panic was the last thing Elms heard before the darkness closed in. Again.

30.

I love her. I love her not. I love her. I love her not. I love her. I love her not. I love her. - Random Thought # 1357

~~

Simon stood in the choir room of the church and adjusted his tie in a small mirror on the wall.

"Knock, knock," his mother called from the doorway.

"Hi, Mom. Come on in."

"I can't believe you're mating today," she gushed. "I thought you'd resist it." Her laughter echoed in the room as she hugged him hard. "Your father was a little put-out that you decided to have Mr. Strom officiate today, though. You might want to talk to him before the ceremony."

"I will." He returned her hug and placed a kiss on her cheek.

His mother had aged wonderfully. She didn't look close to the sixty years she was, except for the grey hairs that she joked were named after him and Siobhan. The joy in her eyes was overwhelming. But every time he blinked, he was plagued with thoughts of Elms instead of his bride-to-be.

"How long until the ceremony begins?"

"Oh, you have about an hour or so. We came early to see if Tiffy's parents needed help getting things ready, but it looks like they've already done the brunt of it. I'll let you finish getting ready, but I'm gonna tell your father to come see you," she warned.

"Sounds good."

When she left, he slumped into a metal folding chair and pulled his phone and headphones from his jacket pocket. He plugged in the ear piece and tucked the ear buds into his ears. He scrolled through the icons on the face of his phone and tapped the music icon. His favorite playlist wasn't there anymore. In its place was a list called 'Little Wind.' Curious, he tapped the words and a familiar tune started. He clicked through a few more songs; all familiar. That was odd. He must've renamed his playlist.

"Son?" His father plucked an ear bud from his ear. "Your mother said you wanted to speak with me." He let the bud fall, dangling by Simon's shoulder.

"Dad," Simon clicked the music off and put the phone and accessories back in his jacket pocket, "thanks for coming today."

"Of course. I'm not going to lie. I really expected you to fix this situation that you're in here." He turned a chair around and sat in it like he was still a teenager instead of nearing sixty-five.

"I did." Confusion flooded his head, removing all thoughts of the redheaded Wind. "I told Tiffy I'd mate her and I took a bottle of Forget."

"Well, it must not've worked if you remember taking it, son." His dad was a pro when it came to judgmental looks and the one he was leveling on Simon right now was one of his finest.

"It did. The Wind I told you about, came here yesterday and kissed me." His sheepish words transported him back to his youth. He couldn't lie to the man who'd given him life. "Now that I remember, it's like I'm living this double life. She runs through my mind and yet here I am, counting down the minutes until I'm expected upstairs to marry someone else. Someone I don't want to hurt, but someone who I can't imagine spending every day of my life with when I can't stop thinking about another woman. What the fuck is wrong with me?"

"Simon, listen to me and listen closely. If you truly believe you are supposed to mate Tiffy, then you should mate Tiffy. But if this other woman, the Wind, is who you think you're meant to be with, then you need to speak up now before you do something you'll regret. Think about it." He patted Simon's leg and stood. "Whatever you decide, your mom and I will stand behind you."

Simon watched his father leave. The walls of the room were closing in on him. He needed space. To breath. To think. To make a decision that he could live with. The basement door of the church was straight ahead. Rather than go through the upstairs and risk running into anyone, he slipped through the door and used his phone to light the darkened stairs that led to steel Bilco doors. With a hard shove, the doors opened under the weight of snow. He slunk around the back of the church like an escaped convict and sprinted across the parking lot. His car shone like a beacon in the rising sun and he aimed right for it. Behind the wheel, he clicked the power on enough to lower the windows. The cold air tugged at him easing the tension from his overheated body.

How was he supposed to do the unthinkable? If he walked into the church and told Tiffy that the wedding was off, he was sure his sister would never forgive him. She was depending on him to mate so she could find hers. And if he did marry Tiffy and they moved to Long Island, what would happen to Elms? Would the distance between them douse her in pain and unrest? She didn't deserve a life of torment like that. And if he stayed here with Tiffy, what would that do to him? Seeing Elms around town would be his undoing. Goddess forbid she started seeing someone. His stomach twisted at the thought. The rules said what was between them was wrong. No. Impossible. But the ripping in his heart told him Fate had played her hand and Elms would forever be his one and only. Unless...

A car screeched into the parking lot and pulled up to the front steps of the church. A short, older woman dashed from the car like Satan himself was nipping at her heels. Puzzled, Simon eased out of the safety of his car and went to follow her. As he neared the car, a flash of red caught his eye. Elms. Slumped in the backseat was the woman he loved. Seeing her pale and twisted in pain confirmed with his head what his heart knew to be true. He loved the Wind. A commotion rose behind him from the front doors of the church, but all he could focus on was Elms.

He wrenched open the door and gathered her too-hot body into his arms. Something was seriously wrong here. As a Wind, she normally felt cool to the touch, but now she was an inferno of heat. He carried her to the snow beside the parking lot and laid her petite body in it, hoping to cool her.

"Simon. Don't touch her." Siobhan's shrill voice rang in the air. "Don't you dare touch her." She seethed again when she reached his side. "This is what you needed, Si. She's going to be out of the picture for good and you and Tiffy can be together."

The look on his sister's face was one he'd never seen before. Pure malice stared back at him. He'd done this to her. He'd driven his sister to do

something unthinkable all because he didn't have
the guts to tell her he loved someone
unconventional. And now Elms was going to pay
the price.

"Shiv. What did you do?" He grabbed her
arms and shook her when she refused to answer. A
crowd formed around them, and the woman he'd
seen running into the church pushed her way
through and ran to Elms' side.

"Are you Simon?" Clipped words flew from
her mouth as she bent to feel his Wind's forehead.

"I am."

"She's been poisoned with flame azalea. She
begged me to bring her to you. She said you'd know
what to do." Tears streaked down the woman's face
and landed on Elms.

"Flame azalea? Shiv, please tell me you
didn't." But the moment he met her eyes, he knew
it was true. Shit. The amorous flower was like
catnip to Fires, but in anyone else, it acted as an
arcane antigen, silently and effectively killing those
who ingested it. His father knelt beside him.

"You can reverse the affects, son, but only if
you hurry."

"How?"

"Trust her instincts. She came here to you;
the man she loves that has turned her away at every
opportunity. Embrace her and let the love you have
for each other consume the toxins. I believe in
you." He leaned closer to Elms and put his ear to
her chest. "Hurry. She doesn't have much time."

Simon cradled Elms in his arms. She felt so

tiny and fragile. He strode through the crowd, into the stone church, and took the steps to the basement with caution, careful not to jostle the woman in his arms. As he rounded a corner, he collided with the one woman standing in the way of a future with Elms, and she was wearing a dress that looked like flaming taffeta.

"Tiffy, move. I have to save her."

"I know. You were never really mine. I wanted to make it work between us. To conform. But seeing you with Elma makes this decision that much easier." She moved aside. "Please forgive your sister. She only wanted you to be happy, and your forgiveness will mean the world to her."

"I can't think about that now, Tif. Elms needs me." He pushed past her, rounded the corner, and entered the choir room. He laid on the floor and curled Elms in his embrace.

"Elma isn't the only one. I need your blessing, Simon."

He glared at his fiancé. "My blessing? What the hell do you need it for?"

"I think I'm in love with your sister," she whispered the words from the doorway, shame etched on her face. "The community will forbid it, but I think I knew the night I first met her that she was the person for me. I've been fighting it for so long that it nearly was my undoing. If I'd just spoken up, we wouldn't be in this mess." Tears streamed down her face.

"You have it, now shut the door and don't let anyone in here until I say so."

The door clicked into place and voices could be heard from the hallway behind it, but he didn't care. He unsnapped the metal tabs holding the hospital issued gown together and worked it off Elms' body. Her skin was flushed with the force of the heat that was burning her from the inside out.

"Little Wind, can you hear me? I need to cool you off. Okay?"

"Simon?"

"Yeah, babe, I'm here. Tell me how to help you."

A smile curled her lips and a sigh escaped between them. "I'm sorry I can't stop loving you. I tried, but I can't."

"I know. I can't get enough of you, either. But, I need you to tell me how to stop the toxin. Please," he begged.

"Just hold me. Let your heat warm me, I need to feel you next to me one more time."

He shrugged out of his jacket, whipped off his shirt and tie, and discarded the thin gown stuck to her body. He pulled her against his bare chest and kissed at every bit of her he could reach. "Please, babe. Tell me what to do."

She tilted her head to meet his lips with hers. The heat inside of her jolted between them when her tongue swept inside his waiting mouth. He nipped at the tip then soothed it with his own, the power of the toxins thick in her saliva acted as intended to his Fire nature.

Powerless against the plant's seductive properties, he sank his tongue into her again, scorching her mouth with his as his hands tugged at the buckle on his belt. Every passing second culled the urge to ravish her. The nectar of her mouth was only an appetizer to whet his hunger. He pulled away from her long enough to shed his remaining clothes and returned to her, a fever ignited in his veins. He licked his way from her neck to her navel and all the places in between, collecting her essence along the way. A soft moan ripped from her throat when he swirled his tongue inside the adorable indentation of her midsection.

The simple sound spurred him on, until he found the apex of her thighs beneath his hungry mouth. He opened her to him and inhaled the sweet scent of her. Sweat beaded on her skin and sizzled into curls of smoke. The fire within him ravaged his nerve endings and burned the slim grasp he had on his sanity in her presence until it snapped. He buried his face into the core of her, lapping at the sweet nectar between her folds until the urge to claim her took hold. His erection hung heavy between his legs and throbbed with want. He needed her, but it would change everything.

"Elms, look at me." When her eyes flickered to meet his, he held his breath then asked, "Are you ready? Because once we do this, there's no going back. You'll be stuck with me."

"Forever?"

"Forever." It was an oath he would be thrilled to keep.

"Promise?"

"With my whole heart, I swear to you."

She smiled and shivered. "Yes." It was a whisper of a word. Her lashes fluttered shut and he could see the color draining from her face.

He wasted no more time. Rocking his hips, he buried himself as deep as her body would allow. The fire within him exploded and enveloped them both in his heat. A saner version of himself would be concerned that his heat would kill her, but instinct took over and her moans of pleasure pushed him over any plateau blocking his path to finding her passion. Her legs wound around his hips, anchoring him to her while she met each of his movements with shudders of satisfaction. Her skin sizzled when it slid against his and her breathing stuttered, but she dug her nails into his back, clinging to him with every bit of strength she possessed. Spasms gripped him tight. He basked in her beauty as heat whipped through him. He pressed his lips to hers and together the flames overtook them and sent them into bliss only true mates could know.

The afterglow was short-lived. Elms' temperature returned to normal in the wake following his climax. Relief flooded his system and the voices beyond the door grew louder. A knock on said door gave him the needed push to roll off his mate. His. Ecstatic, he smiled down at the Wind of his dreams and pulled on his slacks.

"What's the smile for?" Her coy words and the remaining influence of the azalea in his system tempted him to remove his pants and take her all over again.

"I just realized you're mine." His smile stretched wider across his face.

"Pretty sure you're mine," she rebuffed, a laugh in her words. "Hey, is it me, or are they getting loud out there?"

"Not just you, Little Wind." He plucked his shirt off the floor and handed it to her. "Put this on and let's go face the music."

He studied her every move as she slipped the shirt over her shoulders and buttoned every button. His shirt looked amazing on her; long enough to cover the important parts, but sexy and alluring all rolled up in one. He pulled her into his arms and kissed her until life stirred back into the part of him that begged to be buried deep within her again.

"Oh no you don't, Fire Guy. We need to go out there," she chastised. "It's bad enough your sister tried to kill me."

He let her worm from his embrace but snatched her hand before she scooted out of his reach. "We go together." He dropped a quick kiss on her head then opened the door.

Her aunt was the first to push through the throng of angry faces and accusing voices that awaited them.

"Elms? Are you okay?"

"Oh, Sue, thank you." Elms left the safety of

his side and flung herself into her aunt's arms.

"Will someone please tell me what's going on in here?" Isaac Strom waded through the sea of people. "Mr. Foster, what in tarnation is going on down here? We are supposed to begin in ten minutes."

"I'm sorry, but the mating isn't going to happen. At least not with Tiffy and me. Elms and I have bonded. I apologize for wasting your time, sir, but the ceremony is canceled."

"You do realize that it's impossible for a Wind and a Fire to mate, right?"

"Well, sir, we beg to differ." Simon stuffed his hands in his pockets and struggled to find the words that would convince the only person who could bless his bond. "Sir, I tried to resist the attraction between us, so much so that even though I knew in my heart that she was the only person for me, I turned her away. I sought you out and planned to marry the person I was being told was the one for me, when really I should have been on my hands and knees begging you for Elms' hand." With that, he reached for the woman he loved and grabbed her hand tight in his. "Sir, you can tell us 'no,' but I'll take her to the end of the farthest corner of the Earth if I have to be with her."

"Si, you can't." In a whirlwind of gold silk and lace, Shiv pushed Elms aside. "If you don't mate properly, then you doom me to never finding my mate." Fat tears poured down her face. "Please, Si. Don't do this. For me."

"Your mate's already found you." Tiffy's

voice broke the silence. The sea of people parted, letting her through. "I gave your brother my blessing and I wish you would, too." Tiffy stepped closer to Shiv. "I knew we weren't meant to be together, because the person I wanted isn't someone who the community would approve of either. But seeing Elma and Simon together, vulnerable, but in love, I can't keep quiet." His ex-fiancée laid her hand on his sister's cheek and drew her close. She leaned in, whispered some unknown words in her ear, then planted her lips squarely on Shiv's.

The collective gasp was deafening, but what surprised him the most was his sister's reaction. The prim and proper sister who talked non-stop about wanting a husband and a family of her own, grabbed Tiffy around the waist and melted into her. The two women emerged, breathless, when Isaac cleared his throat.

"I see we have some discussions to have, but this isn't the place for it." He nodded to the surrounding townsfolk. "Let's head back to my place and we'll hash this out.

"I can't let you walk out of here."

31.

Mr. D.J., turn it up, it's time to face the music. —
Random Thought # 573

~~

The six-and-a-half-foot mammoth of a man glared at Simon; steel in his eyes.

"Last I checked, you aren't the boss of me." Dammit. Elms pushed herself between him and the giant. His Wind was nothing if not stubborn.

"Elma, you know I have to take her in. She admitted to murder."

"Attempted murder, Charles. That's completely different."

"Elma, be reasonable."

"You know me well enough to know that's

289

not possible."

Simon watched the heated exchange between his mate and the man he'd seen with Elms and her cousin before. She looked fierce; her long hair wild and untamed, eyes blazing with unspent passion brewing behind them, determination furrowing her brows.

"She did what she thought she had to. You know it's true."

"How can you stand there defending her? She almost killed you," he accused.

"Because she was doing what every one of you would do if it was your brother and he was about to mate with someone outside of the community covenants." Her head whipped from one side of the crowd to the other. "We've been conditioned to believe that only a certain way is acceptable, and any time something contrary to that happens, we are conditioned to quash it before it can upset the delicate balance we keep. It's us against the humans, and now us against each other if we can't be open to the idea that we might love someone other than who the community has conditioned us to think we can love."

The hurt radiated off his mate in palpable waves as the words poured from her lips. She wasn't exaggerating; in his lifetime he'd seen many who defied the rules of the community turned away or worse. The full impact of what they'd done hit him square in the chest.

By saving her, he all but insured that she'd lose everything she loved. Goddess, he'd saved her and now they could both be sentenced to banishment or worse, death. His heart clenched and dropped. That was the moment his mate swung back to meet his eyes. Eyes he knew betrayed him. Eyes that would tell her that he was full of regret. Unsure he'd survive her disappointment, he turned from the person he loved more than life itself and rearranged the muscles of his face into what he hoped was a believable show of support. But by the time he was confident enough to meet her stare, he knew the damage had been done. The fire in her eyes was gone and replaced with what he'd come to recognize as the beginning of her Elemental shift. Shit. She was seconds away from shifting and fleeing.

"Don't." The word tumbled from his mouth before she could embrace the change.

"Why? I can feel your regret." Her voice broke and the shimmer of tears caught his attention.

"No, Little Wind. I could never regret saving you. But I can regret the life I doomed you to because I was careless with my love. I remember everything now, and every step of the way, I should've been turning away from you, or at the very least, made myself stay away from you. But I didn't. I let the allure of you drive me to put you in a position that could take everything you ever worked for away from you."

"Until right this moment, I didn't care about any of that. As long as I have you, I know I'd be all right. That we'd be all right." She turned to the man she'd called Charles and poked him in the chest. "I'm not pressing charges, so you have nothing to pursue when it comes to Siobhan." Then she turned to Isaac and did the unthinkable. "Banish me if you think it's what the community needs, but it will only cause unrest that will stretch as far and wide as I travel, because I will make sure that everyone knows that when Fate called me to mate with a Fire, my elder banished me for answering Fate's call."

The strands of her hair began to move on their own and the transition began to take hold.

"Wait for me," he begged. She was right. Fate had tied them together even if they didn't know why, but a bond like what they had wasn't something anyone could force them to break if they didn't want to. He wasn't about to lose the best thing that had ever happened to him.

Simon reached for her hand before it could dissolve into mist. Her transformation halted and she gave him the biggest smile he'd ever seen.

"You didn't think I was about to leave you here all on your own, did you?" Licks of humor tickled her words.

"Not a chance, Little Wind." He hugged her close and dropped a kiss on her head. "You're stuck with me. Let's take you home."

"You do realize the elders will have to vote on your union." Isaac blocked their path through the hall. "I understand the two of you believe you've bonded, but we need proof."

"And how exactly do you think you will

prove our bond is legitimate?" He pulled Elms behind him, ready to protect her.

"Son, there are ways."

The look on his father's face told more than his words. This was going to hurt, and he wasn't about to let anyone else hurt his mate.

"No. Whatever it is, we won't do it. I won't let you."

"Son, think of the alternatives. If Fate truly bonded you, then the community will have no recourse, and I, myself, will perform the mating ceremony."

"And what if we refuse?"

"We'll do it." Elms' breath was warm on his arm. "Since I'm a healer and will be able to sense his distress, you need to use me." She leveled a look at Isaac.

"You don't have to do this." Simon's heart raced and thoughts tumbled through his head faster than he could catch them. "I know you want their blessing, but I won't let them hurt you."

"You and I both know it's the easiest way. I'll be okay. Have some faith."

Her smile would haunt him until they could be together again.

"I'll stay here and report my findings," offered his father.

"That will be fine," agreed Isaac. "Elma, come with me, please."

His mate nodded, but before she left, she wound her arms tightly around him and placed a kiss on the skin covering his heart. A whisper caressed his skin and the words, "I love you," tickled his ears. She caressed his face and followed the elder from the room.

His heart thundered in his chest. The idea of anyone harming his mate was too much to take. The constant heat that simmered in his bloodstream spiked to a boil. The licks of flame on his skin should've been enough to make him calm down before someone got hurt, but he was tired of worrying about what everyone else thought. That's what had gotten him into this situation in the first place. He was here because his family thought he needed to find his mate, and then he fought his attraction to his mate because his community thought he should only mate a Fire. Now he was supposed to stand by and let someone hurt his mate because they thought it was the only way to prove that they were bonded in the way of their people.

The licks of flame became full-fledged bursts of fire on his skin. If he didn't calm down, he would become a full-fledged fireball. An angry fireball at that. And anger made a Fire unpredictable. He'd managed to live this long without that happening, but if there was ever a time for him to nuclear, it was now. He could hear the worried words of his father and other people, but they meant nothing. He was burning out of control and the further away Elms got from him, the more he wanted, no needed, to get to her. He closed his eyes and tried to find her along the thin strands of the bond that connected them now.

He could sense her presence in the church. Like he'd seen her aura before, he now could feel the colors of it in his mind. She was fine. Nervous, but unharmed. He locked onto the beacon that was his mate and concentrated.

A skip in her heartbeat was his undoing. Without another thought, he embraced his nature and was off to rescue his mate. He shifted until he joined the air currents that surrounded him and was only aware of his consciousness. The play of air molecules meshed with his own and soothed him like never before. The heat he was so accustomed to, dissipated. Something wasn't right.

He could still sense Elms, but what he felt filled him with joy. He opened his senses and was confronted with the rushing of a familiar opal gust of wind. In his mind's eye he saw it mingle with a cloud that looked like the red of a sunset on a summer night. The two mingled, swirled, and somersaulted until there was no way to tell where one began and the other ended.

"Does this mean that if I get angry I might burn the place to the ground?"

Her question drifted through the ether and merged in his consciousness until he could hear her sweet voice speaking.

"I hope not." The laughter he felt bubbled up within him and exploded into a blast of heat in his new Wind form.

Elms materialized in her human form complete with his dress shirt as Isaac strode into the room. Reassured that this would be enough to prove to the elders that the two were bonded, he concentrated on regaining his human form.

The flutter of his clothes emerged, too. Just not on his body.

The elder cleared his throat and a good number of the community members had the decency to look away.

Elms winked. "Don't worry, it takes practice."

He grabbed his mate and plastered himself against her tiny body. "Who says I didn't do it on purpose?" The sight of her in his shirt sent the blood in his body all racing below his waist.

"What I just witnessed was enough to convince me." His father's voice jolted him from thoughts of scorching the damn shirt right off Elms' perfect body.

"Agreed. I declare them mated and bonded in the way of the ancients," Isaac added.

"Good, now will everyone give me and my new bride some privacy?" A growl ripped from his throat and Elms chuckled softly against his chest.

His father was the last through the door and closed it with a soft click.

"What's so funny?"

"You, Fire Guy." She laughed in earnest this time.

"Ah, you'll pay for that, Mrs. Fire Guy," he teased.

"Oh, yeah?" She winked and danced away from him. "Who's gonna make me?"

"Oh, Little Wind, if only you knew." He

gave her his most wicked look then flicked a small flame at the hem of the oversized shirt. It landed with a flourish and seeped up the material covering her leg.

A gasp slipped from between her lips and she froze in place.

"Simon?"

He quirked a brow and sent another flicker of flame toward the bottom button. It landed with the precision of a well-trained archer's arrow and singed the delicate thread holding the button in place. The plastic disk, rendered useless, fell to the floor. He repeated the process, button by button, until his fire-haired beauty was surrounded by smoldering pieces of fabric. He was certain the heat in her eyes matched his own.

"Do you trust me?" His voice was thick with want even to his own ears.

"Always." Spoken on a breath, it was all he needed to hear.

He flicked small flames at the remaining seams on the singed garment so that it fell away from her body, leaving her blissfully bared to him. A small shiver overtook his mate. He called another flame to life on the tips of his fingers. Her eyes studied his every motion. He tossed this flame in a less direct route and enjoyed the play of emotions that tumbled through her aura before the flame landed on his intended mark, the bulls-eye peak of her right breast.

A soft groan encouraged the next flame to land south of the first one. The next three followed in pursuit. Each landing closer and closer to the promised land of his salvation. He watched the flames dance on her skin, tantalizing her nerve endings, while he stood back and watched her rapture, the seductive curls of smoke begging him closer.

He stalked his prey, his mate, his true love, unable to contain his desire any longer and knelt before her. He licked at each flame, extinguishing it with his tongue and sending shivers down his spine. His cock jutted thick and heavy from between his legs, begging for a taste of her perfection. He ignored the demands and continued to lavish every nook and cranny of her body with his tongue.

Their previous couplings had been frenzied and he refused to allow this first time as a mated pair to be just another heat-induced fuck. He'd take his time and enjoy learning every blessed inch of his Little Wind, even if it killed them both.

At least that was his plan, until he laved at the sweetness between her legs. The ripple of hair cascading overhead as she shook her head and anchored him to his spot, ignited the fire within, and tossed all thoughts of sweet lovemaking from his mind.

"Mm, mm, more," she panted.

He greedily obliged and swirled his tongue around the tiny bud at her apex. The moan and scrape of fingernails on his scalp nearly drove him mad. He paused his ministrations, sat back on his heels, guided her legs over his shoulders, and secured her to him with strong arms supporting her back.

Little protests fell on deaf ears. Her scent surrounded him and her weeping pussy demanded his attention. He buried his face into the center of her, his tongue snaked through her folds, and lapped against the rippled ridge of her most sensitive spot.

She shattered on a scream of pleasure, then sank, boneless, against him for support. He guided her onto his lap and kissed every inch of her sleepy face.

"I know you must be tired after your ordeal, but Goddess help me, I can't get enough of you." The confession slipped through his lips before he could stop it.

"Show me," she whispered in his ear as she rose enough to situate herself over his erection. With a wicked gleam in her eye, she took him in her folds and buried him to the hilt. "And don't stop until we pass out."

He caught her scandalous lips in his and did as she asked. All day long, in that choir room.

EPILOGUE

Hey, baby! - Random Thought # Oh, who's keeping track anymore?

∿

Elms rolled out from under the comfortable weight of Simon's legs. The past week had slipped by in a blur of ecstasy and excitement. The familiar and welcome soreness in her legs brought a smile to her face. If this was what being mated was like, how did anyone in the community ever get anything accomplished? She and Simon had spent most parts of every day, since their impromptu mating, in bed. Not that she minded a single bit, but today they had to find a permanent place to live.

Sophie had been kind enough to offer them

her home for a while, as long as Elms would take over the day to day responsibilities of the healing center. When they had finally connected, Sophie was quick to explain that her daughter had unexpectedly come into her Elemental gifts and was having some issues. With Elms' blessing, she decided to stay in North Carolina a while longer to help Gracie adjust to her new gifts.

Regardless of what Sophie said about the situation, Elms wondered if she was holding something back. She knew that it was rare for Gracie to develop gifts being that she was a half-breed, but Sophie seemed intent on keeping Gracie in North Carolina rather than bringing her home to Harmony to help with the transition. It boggled her mind that her mentor and friend would keep something from her, but Elms could wait. It would only be another week or so until Sophie was home and then she'd drag whatever had her concerned out into the light of day.

She ambled down the stairs, stifling a yawn and turned into the sunlit kitchen. The kettle called her name from the stove burner, and a tray held two cups and her favorite can of loose-leaf tea. It was a welcome sight in the morning. Simon must've readied it before falling asleep last night, or was it this morning? She smiled and clicked the burner on. Another yawn tugged at each tired muscle in her body.

While the water heated, she settled herself at the kitchen table. The solid wood of the chair was cold against her bare bottom, but it didn't bother her enough to make her move from that spot. It was the incessant buzzing of her cell phone vibrating on the counter that finally encouraged her to move her tired body, but only because she knew the relator would be calling this morning with a schedule of potential houses for the day.

The cold floor teased her feet with every step she took. Ever since taking on some of the Fires' nature, she was surprised how different temperatures affected her. She reached the phone on the third ring and answered without a glance at the caller ID.

"Hello?"

"Is this Elma McMillan?"

"Yes. May I ask who this is?"

"Hi, Elma. My name is Stephanie. I'm a nurse practitioner at St. Catherine's Hospital. I'm calling because you left against medical advice and we've been trying to get in touch with you for a while now to follow-up."

Ugh, she'd intentionally missed every call from the human hospital ever since the day Sue had walked her out.

"I'm fine. Fully recovered even. Thanks for calling," she offered, hoping it would be enough to get the woman off the phone and the calls to stop.

"I'm glad to hear that, but I need to tell you that something showed in your lab work," the woman continued.

"Oh, I'm sure it's nothing and it's better as well," Elms answered. The kettle whistled from the stove. "Thanks again for the call," she began, in a last-ditch effort to get the woman off the phone.

"You're pregnant," the woman interjected. "I'm not sure if that's what caused your illness, but being that you were pregnant when you were here, you might want to consult with your family physician to check the health of the baby."

Then silence. Blissful silence.

"Are you still there, Ms. McMillan?"

"Are you certain?"

"Very much so."

"Okay. Thank you." She clicked off the phone even though the woman was still talking on the other end. The kettle whined in heated protest, but all she could do is run her fingers over the skin of her stomach. It was still smooth and taunt, but soon it would bulge to make room for the little being growing inside.

The noisy kettle quieted and a large palm slid between her hands on her stomach.

"Did I ever tell you how much I love walking into a room and finding you wearing nothing but your skin?" Simon's breath tickled her neck as he spoke. He slid his equally bare body across her back and drew her softness against his hardness. "Let's go back to bed, the tea can wait."

The feel of him, hard and ready, brought a smile to her lips, "As long as you don't mind a threesome, Fire Guy."

THE END

ACKNOWLEDGEMENTS

I always have a long list of people to thank, and every time I feel I only get the very tip of the iceberg.

As always, thanks to Ron, E, and A for thinking I am the best mom ever. Every day that I have with you is a true blessing. I'm fortunate to have such an amazing family. Thank you to my in-laws for helping Ron with the kids so I can work. I'm eternally grateful to you both.

Thank you to all of my amazing writing and critique partners (N.R., D.L., R.P., J.S, S.H., E.R., A.M., D.M.W., & T.P.).

To Reagan Phillips, Denise Leton, and N.R. Ratcliffe, I keep saying I couldn't do this without you and it's truer every time I write it. A special shout out to Natalie for reminding me that I'm the writer and can make whatever book I wanted be the first in a series.

Also, a huge 'thank you' to all the members of Carolina Romance Writers. This wonderful group of writers is uplifting, supportive, and comforting. There will never be a writing group as fun and exciting as you guys.

A huge 'thank you' to Lara Stokes, Jamie Pejo, Dayanara Lorenzo, and Steven Taylor for reading this book even when it sucked. A special thank you to Darynda Jones for critiquing the opening and telling me she believed in the book. Your kind words were the push I needed to put myself and the book out there. I will always be eternally grateful to you.

Thanks to all the amazing people at Rush Espresso who put up with my decaf habit and are always quick to smile even before I've had my first sip. You guys rock.

A huge 'thank you' to everyone who helped edit. Especially Jan Carol and Joshua Strecker. Without these amazingly talented professionals, I'd be in a padded room, still wondering where the commas go.

With all my thanks,

~ j

HOOKED?

~

Want to know what will happen next in Harmony?

Visit www.jeniburns.com to learn more.

Jeni loves hearing from readers.

Reach out to her on social media or leave her a review.

Thank you!

BIOGRAPHY

Jeni Burns is a Jersey girl living in a southern world. While she's firmly planted in the South with her husband, two kids, and one massive poodle, her heart still lives in the Northwestern part of New Jersey where her characters reside. Since writing about home is cheaper than airfare, she spends much of her time living vicariously in NJ's snowy winters and humidity-free summers.

Jeni has been telling stories since she first learned to string two words together. Thanks to her mom and her middle school English teacher both telling her she should be a writer, she now happily spends her days writing all the stories that continuously float around in her head while drinking fabulous decaf coffees.